Yakimali's Gift

Yakimali's Gift

LINDA COVELLA

LINDA COVELLA

Printed in the United States of America

First Printing, 2014
This edition, 2015

ISBN-10: 0692579834
ISBN-13: 978-0-692-57983-1

Cover design by Tugboat Designs
Interior by Jo Michaels of INDIE Books Gone Wild

Praise for Yakimali's Gift

"Well researched and beautifully told, Yakamali's Gift is a literary treasure. Historical fiction buffs will delight in Linda Covella's depiction of Yakimali and the eclectic group of travelers who join her on her journey. Rich in culture, and resplendent with vivid depictions of the arduous trek embarked upon by these spirited travelers, Yakimali's Gift is sure to be loved by readers young and old. Recommended for home and school libraries."

~Literary Classics

Yakimali's Gift received the Literary Classics 2015 Gold Medal for Young Adult Cultural Issues and their Seal of Approval.

"What a delight! Set in 1775, Yakimali's Gift shines light on a little-known part of history and invites the reader to experience it first hand. Ms. Covella does a beautiful job crafting a three-dimensional story that brings the reader on a colorful cultural adventure. The feel of the material, the smell of the fires, the anticipation of the unknown, the sorrow of loss, the sensations of first love—all await the reader of Yakimali's Gift. Armed with her engaging story, Covella invites the reader to step into a time gone by and live it."

~ Sofia St. Angeles of InD'tale Magazine

Yakimali's Gift won the 2015 RONE (Reward of Novel Excellence sponsored by InD'tale Magazine) Honorable Mention for General Young Adult.

"Covella's extensive research into the culture and society of the Spanish-settled New World is worked seamlessly into a very human story in which Fernanda's quest to understand her mother's Pima ancestry gradually takes center stage."

~ Teresa Devine of the Historical Novel Society

Dedication

Dedicated to my mother, Mary Covella, who taught me to love all forms of art, including books, who is my biggest supporter in all things I do, and who is the best mom anyone could dream of having.

In memory of my brother, Michael Covella, who always asked about my writing and who always told me to never give up. I love and miss you, Mikey.

Acknowledgements

First, I want to thank my readers. You're the reason I spin my stories. I hope with *Yakimali's Gift* you're transported to another time and place while finding something of yourself in Fernanda's story.

I'd like to send a very big thank you to my amazing critique partners: Dale Ibitz, Chrissie Pollock, Mary Beth Schewitz, Linda Stanek, and Jen Funk Weber. You gals are wonderful writers, sharp critics, and great friends. *Yakimali's Gift* wouldn't be the story it is without you!

Thank you to my other critique partners Nathalie Mvondo, Mike Purfield, and Lisa Franco who helped me dig deeper into character and plot. Your input and feedback were invaluable.

Last, and most important, I want to thank my husband, Charlie Allan. Because of his hard work, I'm able to fit in time for my writing, and I wouldn't be here without his love and support. I know how lucky I am to have the best husband and best friend I could ever hope for!

Also by Linda Covella

The Castle Blues Quake
Book One in the Ghost Whisperer Series

The Ghosts of Pebble Brook Lodge
Book Two in the Ghost Whisperer Series

Contents

Part One:

Life in Mexico, New Spain

August – October 1775

Chapter One

Fernanda pressed her heels into the horse's sides. "Faster, pretty one, faster. We want to feel the wind in our hair, no?"

The horse flicked its ears then galloped across the plain toward the river, kicking up stones from the hard ground. Fernanda leaned closer to the horse's neck, her long braid slipping over her shoulder. The animal's smell of grassy manure and sweat filled her with the thrill of riding. It had been too long.

Her body rocked forward and back with the rhythm of the pounding hooves. Water streaked from her eyes as she raced across the desert, dodging barrel cactuses and mesquite bushes. Her *rebozo* loosened and slipped to her shoulders; then the shawl untied completely and was gone. Fernanda glanced over her shoulder and saw it flutter to the ground. A laugh burst from her chest, and watching a hawk glide, dive, and then fly high into the sky, she thought, *I feel as free as that bird!*

The power of the horse flowed through her, charging her with the desire for adventure, her heart soaring beyond Tubac to worlds far away, worlds full of golden riches, handsome men, and green hills that rolled on forever. Worlds where she would ride, explore, and each day discover something new.

Before realizing how far she'd gone, she saw her family's adobe hut. She tightened the reins, stopped the horse, and squinted toward the house. Her soaring heart dropped like the hawk diving to the ground. There, in front of the hut with her hands on her hips, stood her mother. Fernanda braced herself against the scowl she was sure to see on Mama's face when she returned. The scolding words she was sure to hear.

Fernanda turned the horse around and headed back to her brother Luis, back to the *presidio* and the market. Keeping the animal at a respectable trot, she clenched the reins. Why did Mama insist that galloping was improper? And why did Papa follow her lead when he knew she had a special way with horses?

She retrieved the rebozo and shook the dust and weeds from the rough cotton weave. Then, stopping the horse in front of Luis, she jumped to the ground and threw the reins to her brother. Ignoring the sound of disgust he forced from his mouth, she marched over to her mule and flung the shawl across the two baskets of vegetables slung over its back.

"I told you to be quick," Luis said. "Nicolas is back from Horcasitas, and I promised I would safely deliver these horses to him." He held the leads of two other horses.

Fernanda eyed in the distance the high adobe walls and closed gates of the presidio, Tubac's military garrison. She was grateful for a chance to ride, and doubly grateful she'd been able to avoid Nicolas. After pressure from him—and Mama—she'd finally promised to set a date for their marriage once he returned from the capital.

"I'm only back this soon because Mama saw me," Fernanda said. "I expect I'll hear her usual lament—" She held her head between her hands and said in a high wailing voice, "Why oh why must my daughter run around like a wild Apache?"

Luis laughed and nudged his sister. "Perhaps Mama is right. After all, a girl can never ride as well as a man."

"And you are a man? At twelve years old?" But the truth was, even though Fernanda was three years older than Luis, someday he *would* have all the privileges of manhood, while she'd always simply be—a woman. She straightened her bodice and dusted off the sleeves of her blouse and her skirt. "You'd best deliver your horses, and I must sell my vegetables or Mama will have another reason to be angry with her wild, troublesome daughter."

Luis climbed onto the chestnut mare Fernanda had ridden, and it shook its head, whinnied, and pawed the ground.

Huh! Fernanda thought. *That beauty was calm enough with me on her back.*

"Oh, I almost forgot," Luis said. "Watch for Nicolas in the plaza. He has an important announcement to make."

"Announcement? About what?" *Madre de Dios! Not about our marriage?*

Her brother simply grinned, his eyes bright with excitement, though not hiding the superior look for the secret he held. He clucked at the horse and, with the other two horses trailing behind, trotted toward the presidio.

Fernanda kicked a stone, sending it skidding after Luis. No matter. She'd learn soon enough. She grabbed the mule's lead rope and led it across the plaza into the midst of the busy market, into the bleats and snorts of goats, sheep, and pigs, the shouts of vendors hawking tools, earthenware, and food, and the bellows of customers haggling over each *peso*. The thrill of the marketplace surged through her as she hurried to her spot next to Señor Rodriguez, the corn vendor. She was ready to barter. Ready to hold her own against the shrewdest sellers. Ready to get the most from the stingiest buyers.

As the afternoon wore on, Fernanda sold most of her goods, including several earthen jars filled with her popular salsa. She bartered for flour and dried beans or collected cocoa beans and even a few *pesos duros*, hard currency not often seen in that part of New Spain. And, hoping the rare treat of a cup of cocoa would sweeten Mama and soften her anger, she purchased some chocolate, cinnamon, and a bit of sugar.

Finally, she was ready to face Señor Rodriguez, who bargained as if each kernel of corn were a nugget of gold. The trading sessions with him required Fernanda's sharpest wits. She approached his stall, and she thought, as she often did with humor and fondness, how his bumpy skin, thick body, and large head reminded her of a Gila monster. Venom was the only thing missing in his resemblance to the desert lizard.

She pursed her lips and picked through the ears of corn. "Did you have a problem with weevils this year, Señor Rodriguez?"

"Weevils? Never!"

Fernanda pressed two fingers over her lips to stop her smile. Upsetting Rodriguez always improved her bargaining position. "I need ten ears today. What will you trade?"

Rodriguez sucked one end of his wiry mustache into his mouth and eyed Fernanda. Then rapid-fire trading ensued until a deal was reached, Fernanda and, seemingly, Rodriguez, pleased.

Rodriguez picked up a cantaloupe he had traded for, held it close to his nose and breathed in its sweet scent.

"A farmer's soul you have, Fernanda Marquina," he said, mellowed now that the bargaining was complete. "A soul that's part of this land and a love of gardening surely inherited from your mother's people."

"The Pimas enjoy gardening?" Since Mama spoke little of her Indian ancestry, Fernanda savored each morsel of information that came her way.

"Farmers since ancient times. When I was a boy living up north, theirs was always the best produce."

A boy ran past, shouting, "A soldier will read a proclamation from the king!"

"What's that about?" Rodriguez asked.

"I'll find out, if you'll please watch my goods." She grabbed her rebozo and threw it around her shoulders.

"I'll expect a full report when you return."

"*Gracias*!" Fernanda sprinted toward the crowd that had gathered at the other end of the plaza, and hovered at its edge. The gates to the presidio opened, and Nicolas trotted out astride his prancing horse. Three girls, ones Fernanda knew well, looked up at Nicolas with shining eyes. One of the girls, Ramona, spoke to him, smiling in what she most likely thought was a beguiling manner. Fernanda's chest burned. Ramona, with her ever-sharpened talons, would snatch him from Fernanda if she could.

Yes, he's handsome as ever, Fernanda thought. Few men looked as graceful and in command as Nicolas when sitting straight and proud on his prized buckskin horse. The black waves of his hair were combed close to his head and tied into a neat braid. His red uniform was unwrinkled, the breeches hugging the lean muscles of his thighs, the jacket showing off his trim waist and sharp posture of his shoulders.

He tugged the bottom of his leather jerkin, the vest all soldiers wore as protection against Indian arrows, and spoke briefly to the girls. Fernanda relaxed. No smile touched the firm line of his mouth, or lit up his dark eyes, or softened the defined lines of his profile.

As usual, he only cared about the duty at hand. He pulled a document from beneath his vest and called out, "Attention citizens of Tubac. This proclamation, officialized on July 23, 1775, states that the most excellent Viceroy Antonio María de Bucareli, speaking in the name of his Excellency King Carlos the Third, has ordered Captain Juan Bautista de Anza to accept recruits for an expedition to California for the purpose of land settlement and claims for the kingdom of Spain."

Questions, comments and shouts erupted from the crowd. Fernanda was as surprised as the rest. Another expedition to California. But why such an announcement? Expeditions were for soldiers, for men, for the lucky ones.

"Silence, silence," Nicolas yelled.

Fernanda smothered a quiet giggle with her hand. Nicolas hated to be interrupted.

The voices fell mute, and he continued. "For this expedition, men, women, and children are being recruited." Now the people would not be silenced, and Nicolas had to shout the rest of the proclamation. "King Carlos has ordered that each recruit be given all necessary supplies for the journey, including tools, clothing, horses and pack mules. And for each family, a plot of land and provisions for homesteading."

Families going to California! Excitement raced through Fernanda's body. A horse of her own. She would sign on just for that. But new clothes, too? She looked down at the gray petticoat, long ago white, that peeked out from underneath her worn skirt. Her sandals were scuffed and faded, the same color as her dusty feet. The laces on her stained bodice had been replaced a dozen times. And when was the last time she'd worn a ribbon in her hair?

Nicolas called out, "Anyone interested in joining this historic expedition must be listed on the roster tomorrow. That is all."

He scanned the crowd. Fernanda covered her head with her rebozo and scooted behind some men, peeking around them to watch Nicolas. She wasn't prepared to talk to him, knowing what they must discuss. Ramona vied for his attention with her fluttering eyelashes and wiggling hips, but he ignored her. Why couldn't she be thrilled the way Ramona would be if she were betrothed to Nicolas? Though she couldn't imagine him not in her life, she wasn't ready to be a wife, to spend her days cooking and cleaning and serving her husband. Even if he was the most handsome young man in Tubac.

Nicolas looked over the crowd a moment longer then, frowning, trotted back toward the garrison gates. The gathering broke up into small groups, buzzing with talk of the expedition. Fernanda hurried back to Rodriguez and began to gather her things together as she told him about the proclamation.

Rodriguez suddenly interrupted her and said, "Good day, sir."

Fernanda turned around, and there stood Nicolas.

"By luck," he said, "as the crowd thinned, I saw you talking to this gentleman." He bowed stiffly at Rodriguez. And then, his eyes warming as he turned to Fernanda, he said to her, "I have good news. My duties are almost complete for today. I'll be able to come by your house this afternoon or evening. Perhaps it will prove a good time to speak with you, and your father."

Rodriguez' eyebrows rose and one half of his enormous mustache twitched upward in a smile.

Not only embarrassment warmed Fernanda's face, but a feeling of panic, of being trapped, overcame her.

Nicolas threw an irritated look at Rodriguez, said, "Excuse us, Señor," and led Fernanda away from him and other bystanders. His hand still cupping her elbow, he tightened his hold and said, "We must talk. The timing is far more urgent. I'm going on the expedition and it leaves in two months."

Fernanda's stomach knotted, and she looked away.

"Fernanda, you heard the proclamation, didn't you? That families—and married couples—will be joining the expedition? We agreed, did we not, that upon my return from Horcasitas…" When she didn't answer, he said, as if issuing an order, "I must come by this afternoon."

Fernanda's head was spinning. It was all happening too fast. With the expedition looming, Nicolas would insist the marriage happen immediately.

Madre de Dios, she could be a married woman by next week.

Ramona and her friends walked past, their heads tucked together, whispering and giggling, though Ramona boldly stared at Nicolas. Fernanda knew Nicolas was a prize any girl would wish to win, and she had to marry sometime, didn't she? Nicolas treated her well. He promised her a secure life (Mama's oft-repeated reminder). And she would see California, new lands, new people. But how could she leave Papa and Mama and her brothers? As much as her brothers annoyed her, her heart wrenched at the possibility of never seeing them again.

She quickly laid out a plan in her mind. She would convince Papa to go to California. She could use the rich California soil to sell the new homesteaders the choicest produce. And the colonists would be in need of Papa's blacksmithing. Surely he would see the wisdom in that. There'd be more work for him, a future for the boys. And, living on the frontier, more freedom for her.

It only made sense that their marriage wait until they reached California. Mama would support her. How could their married life begin in a tent? She'd make another promise to Nicolas. A solemn promise this time.

Fernanda tossed her head. "Since you insist, Nicolas, you may visit. But I must have time to help Mama with dinner." Then, suddenly guilty because she wasn't being honest with him, she said in a softer voice, "I'll see you later this evening?"

The furrow between his brow disappeared, and his eyes brightened. "Yes, I'll see you then."

Chapter Two

As Fernanda neared her home, a rainstorm burst from a sudden gathering of clouds. The mule stopped. Fernanda tugged on the lead rope. "Come, you stubborn old thing. A little rain won't harm you."

The torrent forced dripping tendrils of hair into her eyes. Puddles formed around her, growing larger as the water beat onto the sun-baked soil. The *tiempo de aguas*, the rainy season, benefited her garden, but it could also bring deluges that lasted hours.

As quickly as it began, the rain stopped. Steam rose from the ground, and the smell of hot moisture hung heavy in the air. She gave the mule's rear a shove. "Go, go! We're almost home." Fernanda grabbed the lead rope; the mule brayed then continued walking.

At the hut, Fernanda tied the mule to a post and set the baskets outside the door. She pulled her rebozo onto her head and knotted it beneath her chin. One less thing for Mama to be angry at, as she insisted Fernanda wear the shawl like a proper woman to keep the sun off her skin and her modesty intact.

Her four-year-old brother Ignacio ran out. "Nanda, you all wet."

Fernanda scooped him up. "Yes, and now so are you." Ignacio squirmed and giggled. Peeking over his shoulder, Fernanda saw her mother standing in the doorway, her hands on her hips, her forehead furrowed, her lips tight. Oh, could Mama find no other way to look at her?

"Fernanda Rosalia Marquina!" Her mother began her litany. "What were you doing riding around like a wild Apache? You're a young lady now. You must settle down." She held her head between her hands. "Oh, why did I ever name you Fernanda?"

Fernanda ducked her head. If Luis were there, they would have burst into laughter. And why *did* Mama name her Fernanda, "the adventurous one"? She may as well be named Inez, "the meek one," for all the freedom Mama allowed her.

Mama continued, "Surely you inherited your wild streak from my grandmother. She, too, insisted on doing things her own way."

Secretly, it pleased Fernanda to be compared to her "wild" great-grandmother. "Mama, you often say that. I do wish I'd known Great-grandmother." She smiled teasingly. "Was she truly as terrible as I?"

"Oh, *Mi'ja*, of course I don't mean you're terrible. It's just that your great-grandmother…she…" A look Fernanda couldn't decipher shadowed her mother's face. Mama shook her head as if clearing an image from her mind. "Sorrowful things happened a long time ago that are best left in the past."

All Fernanda knew about Mama's Pima past was her parents had been killed by Apaches. Suddenly feeling sorry for her, Fernanda rushed to her and clutched her hands. "Mama. I'm sorry about the riding. But the horses were so beautiful.

Luis was bringing them to Nicolas and—" Oh, she should never have mentioned—

"Nicolas? He's back? Did you have a chance to talk?"

Fernanda released her mother's hands and murmured, "These vegetables will rot in the sun."

She emptied the corn from the basket and carried the remaining vegetables into the hut. When she stepped back outside, her mother's hands were again on her hips. She tapped her foot.

"Fernanda?"

"Mama, there's some exciting news. I want to tell you and Papa together."

Her mother clasped her hands beneath her chin and a smile lit up her face. "Exciting news? Perhaps about you and Nicolas?"

"No, Mama. News that's much more important."

"I don't know what could be more important than a young woman having a handsome, responsible man ask for her hand. Especially when that young woman is fifteen. Why, Dolores Sanchez is your age, married, and soon to be a mother. Fernanda, it's time for…"

Fernanda closed her ears to the familiar words. Would her mother never stop pressuring her about marriage? Mama thought Nicolas quite a catch with his thick black hair and light Spanish skin and of course his proper Spanish ways. Nicolas, with his small percentage of Indian blood, could claim the prized and proud name of Spaniard, as everyone throughout New Spain wished to do.

Fernanda glanced at her arm, the brown skin growing darker in the sun. Even though she and her brothers were *mestizos,* half Indian and half Spanish, Mama had been sure to raise them according to Papa's Spanish—and not her Pima—customs.

She heard Papa and the boys behind the hut returning from their day's work. Papa was also pleased with Nicolas, who had known the family since she was a young girl. Somehow the idea that she and Nicolas would marry had evolved into a fact everyone accepted. Including her.

Now, Nicolas, at twenty-one, had gone well beyond his tolerance for waiting.

"Fernanda!" Her father came around the corner of the hut. "How was your success at the market today?"

Fernanda skipped to him and threw her arms around his neck. "I did well, Papa. But the market broke up early. I have such exciting news."

Her father wiped a wet curl from her forehead. "I want to hear your news. First, though, I'd like some dinner. The boys and I have spent the day repairing the fence to keep the jackrabbits out of your garden."

"Thank you, Papa."

She'd wait to tell him. Food would put him in a better mood. She began ripping the husks from the corn, and Mama cocked an eyebrow in surprise. Usually, Fernanda only helped with cooking if her mother coaxed or commanded.

Fernanda's three middle brothers ran from behind the hut and dropped their tools with a clang against the adobe wall. Being so close in age—Antonio 10, Marcos 9, and Jorge 8— they looked alike and were inseparable. With Antonio being the oldest and having the longest name, and Jorge being the youngest and having the shortest name, people were able to remember who was who. And when Fernanda called them her *Hermanos Rábanos*, radish brothers, after carving faces onto a radish with an odd three-lump shape, the name stuck.

"The *culebra de agua* practically washed us away like three tadpoles," Marcos said.

At the mention of the "water snake," Ignacio ran to his mother and buried his face in her skirt.

"This rain was no culebra de agua," Mama said. "We can do without such violent storms." She hugged Ignacio. "Remember, little one. With the rains come the frogs."

She squatted next to a brick oven and started a fire beneath a large pot of water. An awning, made with forked posts and cross-poles laid with branches and reeds, extended out from the hut and protected the oven from the rains. When the water began to boil, Fernanda dropped the corn into the pot.

Another downpour started, and the family hurried into the hut. Fernanda sighed as the cool air skimmed across her hot skin, thankful for the adobe bricks that kept the house cool in the summer and warm in the winter. The hut had three rooms. The Hermanos Rábanos and Luis shared the back room, Mama and Papa slept in the middle room, and the front room served as the family area and Fernanda and Ignacio's bedroom.

Fernanda heard a horse gallop up to the rear of the hut and dashed back outside.

Madre de Dios! Was Nicolas there so soon?

Luis shouted, "Gracias," and ran around to the front.

"Luis, did Nicolas bring you?"

"No, another soldier. Nicolas couldn't come. There was an Apache raid at the presidio."

He ran into the house. Fernanda followed.

"Apaches," he cried again. "At the presidio. They stole horses, maybe five hundred."

Mama pulled him into her arms. "Apaches, those devils! Are you hurt?"

Luis gently pushed away from his mother. "No, Mama. They didn't come into the gates. The horses were grazing outside the presidio, and the soldiers were too late to catch the Indians."

Fernanda sighed with relief. Nobody had been injured. And now Nicolas would be too busy to come and spoil her plan to talk to Papa.

"Why were there so many horses at the presidio?" Papa asked.

Fernanda sucked in her breath. Luis mustn't mention the expedition. Not yet. Let Papa relax, get his belly full...But Luis swaggered over to him.

"I helped Nicolas deliver even more horses today."

"Fernanda," Mama said. "Please fetch the corn."

Fernanda hurried outside, plucked the corn from the pot, and rushed back into the hut. She scraped the corn onto the *metate* and formed a pile of mushy kernels on the flat stone. Grinding the corn into a thick paste, she strained to hear her brother and Papa.

"Add some water, Fernanda," Mama said. "And save some of the corn for tortillas. The rest will be for the *posole*."

"Yes, Mama." Fernanda gritted her teeth, willing Mama to be quiet.

"…and Juan Bautista de Anza has announced a new expedition to California," Luis was saying. "They'll start taking recruits tomorrow; not just soldiers, but families as well."

Papa was looking up, inspecting the twig-and-earth roof that had begun to leak in the rainstorm. "Why would people decide to leave their homeland?" he mumbled.

"But, Papa," Fernanda said. "California is said to be a paradise. Fertile lands and beautiful weather."

"King Carlos will provide the recruits with all they need to make the journey and set up a life in California," Luis said.

"They say they're in need of blacksmiths, Papa," Fernanda said.

"Yes," Luis said. "There's less and less business here, you've said so yourself."

"It's the Apaches," Mama said. "Their looting and fighting are turning people away and ruining our homeland."

"It's not only the Apaches, Mama," Fernanda said. "I can't remember when I was last paid at the market with gold or silver dust. With the mines dried up, people moved to more prosperous places—like California."

"That's true," Luis said. "In California—"

Papa held up his hands. "Stop. You're suggesting we join this expedition? I'll never uproot our family to move to some unknown place. We have all we need right here."

"But, Papa," Fernanda said. "Your ancestors uprooted from Spain and came to this new world."

"And I intend to honor their decision and the life they struggled to make for their descendants. We won't be going to California, and that's final."

Since hearing the proclamation at the plaza, Fernanda had imagined herself already galloping to California. Now, Papa's words yanked the horse right out from under her. She began to form the tortillas, pounding them against the stone with her palm.

"Will Nicolas be going?" Mama asked.

"Yes—" *pound* "he—" *pound* "will."

The tortillas wouldn't hold their shape. Mama scooped up Fernanda's tortilla, rolled it back into a ball, and slapped it between her hands. "Your salsa is delicious; your garden thrives. But your cooking. Ay. You must learn to cook properly if you're to become a good wife someday, and someday soon, I might add. If Nicolas is going to California, we must get busy with the wedding plans."

Fernanda furiously rolled a piece of dough between her hands. She felt as if steam was building in her chest like a sealed pot of boiling water. She'd had enough for one day with Nicolas pressuring her, Papa refusing to join the expedition, and now Mama talking about the wedding as if Fernanda had no say at all in the plans, who she would marry, or how she would live her life.

She threw the hunk of dough onto the metate and stamped her foot. "You'd see me so easily leave my family, my friends, my home? Perhaps I don't want to marry Nicolas. Perhaps I don't want to marry anyone. Perhaps I shall never marry, period!"

Seven shocked faces stared at her. Mama's dark skin turned a shade of lime-washed brick, emphasizing the birthmark on her cheek.

Fernanda glared at her mother. "I can't live the life you want me to, Mama." She turned to run from the hut, but her father's voice stopped her.

"Fernanda." Anger deepened his voice. "Do not speak to your mother with such disrespect. Apologize to her—at once."

Fernanda could still feel the heat in her chest, and her legs pulsed with the urge to run. "I'm sorry, Mama." She knew it sounded hollow and insincere.

The shock on her mother's face had been replaced by a mask that hid any emotions. She turned from Fernanda and continued to prepare the posole.

Fernanda formed more tortillas, her hands like slabs of iron, heavy and lifeless.

The sound of frogs drifted into the quiet hut. Mama and Fernanda carried the food to the oxhide table, and the family sat to eat. Under lowered eyelashes, Fernanda saw that most of her crumbly tortillas were left uneaten. Instead, they concentrated on Mama's delicious posole, the corn cooked into a stew with pieces of dried meat and chunks of sweet potato. For her, though, the food was as tasteless as a bowl of sand.

Later that evening, all except Fernanda gathered outside. She laid a blanket across the table, turning it into the bed she shared with Ignacio. She rested her head on her bundled rebozo, and, in spite of the heat, pulled the lightweight wool blanket up to her shoulder. Curling into its comfort, she felt cloaked in privacy and isolation from her family, something she often craved, but rarely had. Still, the familiar smell of Papa's *cigarro* soothed her.

A dark figure appeared in the doorway backlit by the glow of outdoor candles.

Mama.

Fernanda turned on her side, folded her knees close to her chest, and closed her eyes. The oxhide creaked as Mama sat on the bed. "Mi'ja, will you join us? The stars are beautiful."

"I'm tired tonight, Mama."

Her mother reached across Fernanda's curled body and smoothed her hair off her forehead. "Things can be confusing sometimes, Mi'ja. I, too, once felt as you do. I was younger than you when I married your father. A frightened girl, but also a woman."

Tears burned Fernanda's eyes. Tears at her mother's kind words and gentle touch. But also tears of frustration at her misunderstanding. Fernanda didn't fear marriage. She wasn't a frightened girl, and Nicolas some wrinkled *viejo gordo*. Not that Papa had been old and fat, of course; she just wanted something more. Mama only wanted to do what society dictated, follow rules, do what was expected of her. Whereas she, Fernanda, wanted to live the life *she* chose. Why couldn't she do that? Why?

Oh, Mama will never understand me. Never.

Mama stroked Fernanda's cheek then stood. "Good night, Mi'ja. Sleep well." Her footsteps padded across the hard dirt floor as she left the hut.

Fernanda rolled onto her other side and pressed her face into her rebozo. If only she could escape into the peacefulness of sleep. Usually the croaking of the frogs filled her head with dreams, but tonight they only irritated her. Her anger at Mama returned. Frightened? In fact, she was curious about a husband and wife's relationship, the intimacy between them. If only she could talk to Mama, or someone, about the feelings she'd been having lately, longings in her body for that intimacy.

She rolled onto her back. With her eyes closed, she pressed her forearm against her lips. What would it feel like to be kissed? Remembering how Nicolas's eyes often lingered on her lips, her pulse quickened. Perhaps she would let him kiss her.

The family came into the hut. Mama tucked Ignacio into the bed beside Fernanda, who pretended to be asleep.

When the others had gone to bed, she kissed Ignacio's head, and soon he was breathing deeply. Closing her eyes, she tried to hold back more tears. Of course she would marry Nicolas. She'd only said that to Mama out of anger. But when would she see dear Ignacio, her other brothers, Papa, and Mama again, if ever? She smoothed Ignacio's hair, and a tear rolled into the corner of her mouth.

If she had to leave her family, at least adventure awaited her. The expedition. California. But doubt kept her awake as she pictured herself serving her handsome husband his morning *atole*, and waving as he rode off to explore the hills of California. And later, sitting with the other soldiers' wives, drinking tea, conversing politely about stitching and the best recipe for posole, behaving properly as a good Spanish wife should.

Had she fooled herself thinking life would be different in California?

Chapter Three

The next morning, Fernanda awoke to Ignacio curled next to her whimpering in his sleep.

"*Pobrecito*," she whispered, stroking his cheek. "Everything's fine."

"Nanda," he murmured, rubbing his eyes. "I dreamed the cu'bra agua. So scary!"

"There's no culebra de agua. You heard Mama say so last night. Look, the sun is shining."

But shadows hovered over the bright day when Fernanda remembered Papa's refusal to go to California and her fight with her mother. But her pending marriage dominated her thoughts. She'd tell her parents about her decision after discussing the plans with Nicolas. In the meantime, she promised herself she'd try harder to please Mama. After all, when she left for California, who knew when they would see each other again?

"Come, little brother. I'll make the atole, and we can add a bit of chocolate, and sugar and cinnamon, too."

Ignacio hopped off the bed. "Choc'late!"

After clearing the bed for the morning meal, Fernanda boiled and scraped the corn for the atole. She pressed the kernels through a sieve, ground the mush, emptied it into a pot, and then added water, chocolate, cinnamon and sugar. Her hands worked automatically, her mind on the wedding and the expedition.

Mama came into the room. *"Buenos dias."* She kissed Ignacio, and then checked the atole. "Fernanda, it looks delicious."

"Thank you, Mama," Fernanda murmured. She forced a smile. "I took extra care with it today."

"Very good." Mama peeked out the door. "The sky's as blue as a morning-glory." She began to sing, "This is the bright land, we arrive singing…"

"Don't stop, Mama," Fernanda said. She loved her mother's warm rich voice.

But Mama shook her head and took bowls down from the shelf.

"What song was that?" Fernanda asked.

"A song from my childhood. It's nothing."

Fernanda knew by her mother's firm tone she'd get no more information about the song or Mama's childhood.

Papa and the other boys came into the room and sat at the table. Ignacio scratched his tummy over his shirt. "Mama, I itch."

Mama removed his shirt. "I'll go to the river and wash some clothes."

Ignacio jumped up and down. "I come, I come!"

"Not today, Ignacio," Mama said. "I have too much wash to do to keep an eye on you. Stay with Fernanda and help with her chores."

Fernanda's feet dragged as she carried the bowls of atole to the table. A day full of chores, chores, and more chores. But, placing a bowl in front of Papa, she forced a smile. *I promised I would try. I promised…I promised…I promised…*

Papa drank some atole, and then said to his wife, "Our daughter is learning well." He winked at Fernanda. "There's hope for her yet, I think."

Could they speak of nothing else? "Mama, if the rain returns, the river will swell like a drowned frog. Perhaps you should do the wash tomorrow."

"If the river does rise, it quickly drops once the rain stops. It won't be a problem," Mama said.

Papa stood. "The Rábanos, Luis, and I are off to gather wood to fix this leaky roof."

"Fernanda," Mama said. "You can prepare their noontime meal when they return."

The boys glanced at each other, obviously concerned Fernanda would be cooking their food. She bowed her head over her bowl. If they didn't like it, they could do it themselves. Then, again, thought, *I promised…I promised…I promised…*

After breakfast, the Rábanos formed a line outside the hut with Antonio in the lead. "Soldiers," Antonio said. "Are you ready for your duty?"

"Yes, sir," Marcos said.

"Ready, sir sergeant," Jorge said.

The three brothers raised their stick rifles and marched in a single file behind Papa and Luis.

Fernanda hefted the baskets over the mule and helped her mother load the dirty clothes, the mule braying with each armful.

"Oh, hush, you lazy thing," Fernanda said. "You'll carry this load for Mama and not complain."

Her mother tugged Fernanda's braid. "What does the mule have to say to that, *Mi'ja Querida?*"

Mama considered talking to animals one more of Fernanda's unconventional ways, and in rare playful moments, she teased her daughter. Usually, Fernanda welcomed the teasing, feeling closer to Mama when she dropped her stern exterior. Now, though, she was reminded of all the things she did that displeased her mother. She pulled her braid over her shoulder out of Mama's reach. She'd try harder with the cooking, but she'd never stop talking to mules or horses or any other animals she cared to converse with.

Ignacio came outside waving a shirt. "It itched my skin."

Mama tossed it into a basket. "I'll rinse the clothes extra well today. No more itchy skin, *Mi'jo.*"

If only soap were more plentiful. Instead, they used the crushed fruit of the soapberry tree. The white milky liquid foamed like soap and cleaned well, but their skin itched if the clothes weren't rinsed thoroughly.

Mama yanked on the lead rope and led the mule in the direction of the river. "Fernanda, don't forget the noontime meal." Then she smiled and said, "The atole was delicious this morning."

Fernanda knew Mama was trying to make amends, but their fight the night before still had a hold on her feelings. She murmured, "Thank you."

"Perhaps when I come back we can talk," Mama said.

Fernanda thought how pleased her mother would be if she told her now about the wedding. But first she would discuss the plans with Nicolas. She nodded, her mind on Nicolas, the journey, marriage…She took Ignacio's hand and returned to the hut. At the door, she hesitated and looked back at Mama, thinking to call out to her, to give her a small hint of what they might talk about when she returned. But her mother was trudging determinedly toward the river, and, deciding not to stop her, Fernanda led Ignacio into the hut.

She counted the chores off in her mind: clean the breakfast dishes; string and hang the chilis for drying; weed the garden; make the noontime meal. She brushed the end of her braid across her chin. What could she cook? Perhaps a stew. That would be easy, and if she made enough they could eat it for the noon and evening meals, so she'd only have to cook once.

She eyed the dirty dishes and waved her hand as if they might disappear. She'd string the chilis first—the least disagreeable job—and they could begin drying while she finished the other chores. Using a knife, Fernanda poked a hole in each chili and then showed Ignacio how to thread them onto a leather string.

A hot breeze occasionally wafted into the hut as the morning wore on. Every so often, Fernanda dashed outside to scan the horizon, hoping to see Nicolas on his way to visit her, hoping to speak with him before the family returned. But the desert remained quiet and still except for the high-pitched screech of a hawk or a darting jackrabbit.

She and Ignacio draped string after string across the table until the basket was empty. "Next," Fernanda said, "we must hang them in the sun." Looking around the room, though, she realized she'd accomplished little since starting her chores. Where had the morning gone? She piled the strings of chilis into the basket. She'd hang them later. Quickly, she washed the earthen dishes and laid them on the table to dry. Next she chopped sweet potatoes and carrots for the stew. She'd add some lentils and try to make tortillas again. Surely they'd be an improvement on last night's.

The Rábanos walked into the hut, pushing and jostling each other.

"Antonio," Fernanda said. "Are you all back so soon?"

"So soon? It's time to eat, and we're starving."

Marcos sniffed the air. "Did you cook anything?"

"Where's Mama?" Jorge asked.

Fernanda chopped faster. "I didn't realize it was so late. Is Papa on his way, too?"

"No," Antonio said. "He and Luis are helping Julio Sanchez fix his wagon. Julio will bring them home with the wood."

Fernanda's tense shoulders relaxed. She had time to cook something before Papa came home. A few splatters of rain hit the roof. Soon, a steady downpour doused the tiny hut. "Oh, poor Mama with all that laundry, and Papa and Luis with the wood."

Antonio shrugged. "It'll probably stop soon."

True enough, Fernanda thought.

The boys settled around the table, waiting for their meal. Fernanda plopped the vegetables into a pot of water, and then dropped the lid on with a loud clang. Couldn't they do something to help? She carried the heavy pot out to the stove and lit the fire. Turning to go back inside, a movement in the distance caught her eye. Why, it was the mule. That foolish animal hated the rain and left Mama stranded, unable to bring the laundry home.

I'll take the mule back to her, she thought. *I'll show Mama I truly mean to try harder.*

Back inside, she said, "Antonio, that ridiculous mule left Mama at the river. You three watch Ignacio while I go help her with the laundry." She hesitated. Could they be trusted to take care of Ignacio? If something should happen…well, Papa would return shortly.

"But Nanda," Jorge whined. "What will we have to eat?"

Fernanda pounded her fist on the oxhide table. "Are you a little baby? Can't you see I have to help Mama? The soup is on the stove. Antonio can serve it when it's ready." She whirled away from their horrified faces and stomped from the hut.

Just as the mule walked up, the rain stopped. Fernanda grabbed the animal's lead rope and pulled it toward the river. "You'll return to Mama and carry the laundry home, do you hear?"

Instead of following the road, she cut across the field of rocky soil, hackberry shrub, and devil's claw, thankful the devil's claw's brilliant yellow flowers sprawled before her instead of the sharp hooks of its seedpods. And Mama's favorite blue morning-glories. And orange poppies. All blooming with the August rains. On the way home, she'd pick flowers for a bouquet. Perhaps it would help the family forget they'd eaten vegetable stew for lunch *and* dinner.

Halfway to the river, the sky darkened and showers started again. The downpour increased. Wind buffeted Fernanda, slowing her pace and reminding her of the culebra de agua Ignacio feared. Surely the rain would stop as it had earlier.

The mule halted, and she yanked on the rope. "Come, you old fool! Why did you leave Mama, anyway?" The question made her pause. Mama, more stubborn than the mule, would never have let it get away. Perhaps, in the rain, she didn't see it leave. Fernanda slapped the mule's behind. "Oh, for once will you hurry?" The mule brayed, but started walking.

By the time she reached the cottonwood trees that lined the river, rain was half-blinding her, and her drenched clothes clung to her body. The trees creaked as they swayed in the wind. A gust bent them, straining, over the river. Fernanda wiped water from her eyes and looped the mule's rope around a tree trunk. Lifting her rain-soaked skirt, she ran to the bank that overlooked the river. A few pieces of clothing hung from the branches. Clothes that perhaps earlier flapped in the breeze now hung limp and lifeless. Looking up and down the surging river, she saw no sign of Mama.

Abruptly, the rain stopped. Fernanda scooted down the bank and peered past the trees and overgrown brush. She squinted, and then gasped with relief. Mama! She raised her hand, ready to call out, but dropped it back to her side. It wasn't Mama, only a pile of clothes on a rock near the other side of the river. Foreboding tightened her chest. Where was her mother?

Fernanda stepped onto the nearest rock, looking for the best route to cross the river. It would have been easy before the rain, but now the water boiled over the rocks. She hopped to the next boulder, stepped on her skirt, and tottered. Cursing, she tied her skirt above her knees. She pulled off her sandals and tossed them onto the shore. With her bare feet gripping each rock, she leaped from boulder to boulder, moving farther into the roaring river. Hopping over an eddy, she landed on the flat rock that held the pile of laundry. The large makeshift table rose above the swirling water. *Mama's favorite spot for rinsing the clothes*, a voice whispered in her mind.

Fernanda glanced back to the river's edge, knowing how easily someone could slip and fall. Slip, and be carried away with the powerful current. A strangled cry escaped from her constricted throat. *Mama, where are you?* She swallowed the next sob and set her lips. *She's farther down the river, I know it!*

Still, the other voice said, *Why are the clothes on this rock?*

Fernanda picked up a shirt covered with the milky suds of the soapberry fruit. Her mother's voice echoed in her mind:

"No more itchy skin, Mi'jo. No more itchy skin, Mi'jo. No more…"

Fernanda fingered the shirt while studying the river downstream. Her fingers froze. Just before a bend, close to the bank, she saw a piece of material the same blue as her mother's blouse.

Her heart pounded. She stood and, forcing herself to go slowly, stepped across the boulders. She reached the other side. The river had begun to drop. Pulling the overhanging branches from her path, she waded along the shore. Thorny twigs scratched her bare legs. She stumbled but caught herself, and continued walking. Then a wave of coldness flushed through her body and froze her steps.

"Mama!" she cried. She choked and held her hand over her mouth as she heaved. There, caught in the tangled brush and fallen branches, was her mother. Blood trickled from her forehead into the water, mingling with her hair that swirled around her head. Her face was an eerie white with the green tint of the river flowing over it. Her eyes stared up, unseeing, at Fernanda.

"Maaaamaaaa!" Fernanda screamed. She grabbed her mother under the arms and with incredible strength dragged her onto the bank. She laid her ear against Mama's chest and moaned when she heard no heartbeat. Holding her mother's face between her hands, she shouted, "Mama. Mama!"

But her mother's skin felt so unnaturally cold, so lifeless, she knew Mama was gone.

Fernanda stared up into the tangled trees and, with horror, disbelief, and despair bursting from her chest, shouted, "No! Oh God, Mama, no!"

She collapsed across her mother's body, weeping and moaning, saying over and over, "Mama. Please, God, no. Mama. What will become of us now? How can we live without you, Mama? What will become of us now?"

Chapter Four

Fernanda sat on a log, watching Ignacio dig in the dirt. Three weeks had passed since Mama's death. Fernanda could not rid from her mind the image of her mother in the water. Had Mama suffered? Did she struggle to save herself, hoping someone would come to her aid? Or did she, please God, fall unconscious the minute she hit her head? When her body was lowered into the grave and sprinkled with the white lime that would hasten her return to the earth, Fernanda had turned away. But the scrape of the shovel and the thud of dirt would echo in her head for the rest of her life.

Her shoulders drooped. Her body seemed to be pulled down into the very ground that held her mother. She should prepare the noon meal, but she couldn't raise the energy to stand. No one seemed hungry anyway, and her brothers only complained about the food she prepared. Didn't they realize she was trying her best? Did they ever offer to help? No, of course not. She, the woman, must do everything. Fernanda rubbed her eyes. She shouldn't bicker with them. She should try to comfort them more than she did. Poor Papa needed her help.

She peered up at the roof. The holes had been neglected since that horrible day, and Papa was finally repairing them. He had sat in a chair every day for a week, as if only half-alive, waiting for the sun to set, waiting for another day to pass. Now, at least, he was doing something, although his heart didn't seem to be in it.

The sound of trotting hooves broke into her thoughts. Nicolas rode up, tied his horse to a post, and then sat next to her.

Ignacio called, "Nic'las, look!" He held up a stone, the sparkling fool's gold glinting in the sun.

Nicolas waved, and then caressed Fernanda's hand. "How are you faring?"

She shrugged.

"Fernanda." Nicolas lifted her chin, forcing her to look into his eyes. "I know you have much sorrow. But your family needs your help. You must be the one who brings their lives back to normal."

She jerked her head away. *Always telling me what I must do.* "Why does it have to be me? The boys do nothing to help." She dropped her head onto her lap and began to weep. "I'm not prepared for this. Oh, I miss Mama, I miss her so much."

Nicolas wrapped his arms around her, and Fernanda cried into his chest. They'd never been so close, but the sun-warmed wool of his jacket and the smells it had absorbed—horses, leather, tobacco—comforted her. At least for a few minutes, her mind didn't have to think, her heart didn't have to feel.

Nicolas rubbed his cheek against her hair and murmured, "We'll deal with this tragedy together, my love."

Fernanda wiped her tears with the back of her hand and released a long shaky breath. She gently pushed away from Nicolas. He truly was a good man. She'd never had a chance to talk to him about their wedding plans. And now…

As if hearing her thoughts, he said, "I know, in deference to your mother, our marriage will have to be delayed. I understand, Fernanda, and we have ample time to discuss it before the expedition departs."

The expedition. California. Now it seemed like a silly girl's dream. How could she marry Nicolas and live in far-off California? She couldn't leave Papa to care for the boys by himself. And what kind of life would she lead in Tubac with Nicolas gone, the boys to care for, the house, the chores, all on her shoulders? Guilt washed over her, prickling her skin like dried suds from the soapberry fruit. How could she think about her own happiness and dreams? Poor Papa…her brothers…little Ignacio without a mother…Still, she couldn't help picturing herself trapped inside the small adobe hut, year after year, until she was a gray shriveled old woman.

Unlike Ramona, who had been sure to let Fernanda know her father, a lieutenant, had joined the expedition and her entire family would be going to California. Casually, cruelly, mentioning it at Mama's funeral while sliding glances toward Nicolas. But what did that matter now?

Nicolas was right about her family. She gazed around the yard, trying to see through eyes unclouded by grief. Ignacio's shirt was torn and dirty, his face smudged with dust. The firewood needed stacking. Broken sections of fence left the weed-filled garden unprotected. Flies buzzed around the filthy mule's eyes.

"Yes, Nicolas," she said. "I've been hiding in my sorrow. I must pull the family back together." Her head throbbed with the responsibility, and she forced away more tears. As for Nicolas, she'd talk to him about their marriage—that there would be no marriage—later.

Ignacio shouted, "Nanda, look!" He bounced on top of a boulder, pointing toward the road that ran a short distance past the hut.

Nicolas leaped up from the log. "It's Captain Anza with the recruits from Horcasitas."

Fernanda picked up Ignacio and walked to the fence for a closer look. She glanced up at the roof to see if Papa was watching, but there was no sign of him.

Nicolas joined her. "At long last, they're here," he said. "We'll be setting out for the journey within the month no doubt, sooner with any luck."

Fernanda studied the entourage as they passed, and her heart came alive for the first time since her mother's death. If only Mama were there to see. She bounced Ignacio in her arms. "Look, Nacio! These people will travel all the way to California."

"Cows, too?"

Fernanda pressed her cheek against his. "Yes, the cows, too."

Captain Anza led the travelers, and she had no doubt he was, indeed, Juan Bautista de Anza. He rode high on his horse, his back straight with authority. His entire being seemed to point the way forward: his jutting beard, his intent gaze, his long narrow nose. Three Franciscan priests, dressed in brown, dusty-hemmed robes and sandals, rode with him. Two wore wide-brimmed hats. The third, his scalp shaved except for a ring of hair encircling his head like a halo, spoke earnestly to the captain.

"The priest talking to Captain Anza is Father Pedro Font," Nicolas said. "He's renowned for his knowledge of geography and will record the latitudes and longitudes for the captain." Nicolas snorted. "Yes, a learned man, and he'll be helpful on the journey. But more often a hindrance with his irritating, complaining ways."

"What of the other priests?"

"Fray Antonio Garcés accompanied Anza on the first expedition to Monte Rey in Alta California. On this trip, he and Fray Tomás Eixarch will only go as far as the northern region of the Rio Colorado."

Fernanda's head buzzed with the names: Monte Rey (King's Mountain) and Rio Colorado (Red River), conjuring visions of strange and wonderful new lands.

Nicolas, with soldierly authority, said, "There are approximately 170 people, including families, soldiers, muleteers, and *vaqueros*. The captain hopes to add at least seventy more here at Tubac. There are also three Indian interpreters."

"The colonists will have close contact with Indians?" Fernanda asked.

"Yes, on last year's expedition, the Yumas and Pimas were very helpful to the soldiers."

Pimas, Mama's tribe. Oh, for a chance to see them. A girl Fernanda's age rode past, and she imagined being in the girl's place. If she did meet the Pimas, would she be able to communicate with them? What would they look like? Like Mama? Like *her*?

Nicolas's voice broke into her daydream, relating more statistics. "Those pack mules, 165 of them, carry the provisions. Quite a load with food, tents, arms, and presents for the Indians. The vaqueros are herding more than three hundred cattle and the same number of horses. Half the cattle will be used for food on the journey, the other half for the missions in California."

Ignacio squirmed in her arms, and when she set him on the ground, he waved to the travelers, shouting, "*Hola. Hola*!"

The colonists were not the uplifting parade of adventurers Fernanda expected. They slumped on their horses, swatted flies from their faces, and scratched their scalps. A few of the women appeared to be with child.

Two people stood out, though. A young man and a girl both rode beautiful horses, he a black and she a dapple gray. The girl waved at Ignacio, sidled her horse closer to them, and called, "Buenos dias."

The young man called to her, "Gloria, stay with the group."

The girl hesitated, then trotted up to Ignacio, dug in her saddlebag, and handed him a wooden top. Ignacio took it and stared at it as if it were a golden treasure. Fernanda put her hands on her brother's shoulders. "What do you say, Ignacio?"

"Gracias!" He squatted on the ground and spun the top.

Fernanda smiled at the girl. "That's very kind of you. Tell me, how has the journey—"

"Gloria," the young man called. He rode over to them. His lips were set, his jaw tense, his eyes narrowed. "I told you not to wander off by yourself."

"I only wanted to give this little boy one of my tops," she said.

"You certainly pleased him. Thank you, again," Fernanda said.

Looking at Fernanda, the man's face, for a brief moment, lost its hard edge: his eyes widened, his lips parted.

Fernanda felt her own face grow hot. Her heart skipped, causing her to catch her breath. The man's straight, thick black hair was barely contained in a queue at the back of his neck. Sweat stained his shirt that, though dirty, looked to be of the finest cotton the way it draped over his broad chest and muscular arms.

Then his dark complexion flushed when he seemed to realize he was staring. His full lips closed, again, into a hard line. Fernanda forced her eyes away from his and looked at Nicolas, who was scowling at the other man. Nicolas stepped closer to Fernanda and held her elbow possessively.

The young man glared back at Nicolas, a sneer twisting his mouth. "Come, Gloria," he said, turning his horse sharply, and then trotted back toward the other travelers. Gloria waved goodbye, and then followed him.

"Insolent…" Nicolas mumbled some other unintelligible words as he and Fernanda watched them ride away.

"The girl was so sweet, though," she said.

"Yes, and it will be a long journey for her traveling at the side of that impertinent swine."

Fernanda shook her shoulders slightly, still feeling the man's stare, how it had seemed to grip her, how she'd been unable to look away…

Later that evening, Fernanda lay on her bed with Ignacio in her arms. Papa sat outside as he did every night since Mama's death. Stifled by sadness and heat, hoping Papa would like some company, Fernanda slipped off the bed and tiptoed outside.

Her father sat on a log, staring across the desert, loosely holding his tin cigarette box on his lap. Fernanda slid the box from his hands, opened it, and rolled a cigarro for him. Almost every night, her mother had done the same, presenting the cigarro to him as she would to an honored guest, except for the loving, caressing touch of her hand on his.

Papa took the box from Fernanda and removed the flint, steel, and cotton wick. Holding the cigarro between his lips, he struck the flint against the steel until a spark caught the wick, and he lit the tobacco. In the flare of the fire, Fernanda glimpsed his heavy-lidded eyes. He inhaled deeply then breathed out, letting the smoke escape in a cloud around his head. "Mi'ja," he said, picking up her hand.

"Yes, Papa?" Fernanda tried to peer into his eyes, but they were lost again in the darkness and smoke.

"I watched Captain Anza and the colonists trail past our house today."

Ah, he *had* seen them.

"I thought of the new life they'll have in California." His voice choked, and he dropped his head in his hands. "There's nothing here for us now. I can't face each day, seeing the familiar places, expecting your mother to call us to our meal, to join me here as we talk and gaze at the stars."

"Papa," Fernanda whispered, and touched his shoulder.

He raised his head. "I'm prepared to take the family on this journey. Do you still think that's best?"

The old excitement tugged at her stomach, but it quickly passed. Nothing could replace the hollow, aching feeling of knowing her mother was gone forever. "Whatever you wish, Papa. I'll do whatever you wish."

Papa again gazed out at the desert. "Did you know your mother was fourteen when we met? I was a twenty-year-old soldier in the King's army." A smile twitched on his lips, and he spoke into the night, as if remembering, picturing his past. "I was brash, audacious, apparently handsome to the ladies, and I enjoyed their attention. Then I met your mother when our platoon stopped at the mission where she lived. When I first saw her, the way she was hoeing the soil with strength and determination impressed me. And later, loving her the minute I looked into her dark eyes, those eyes that told me she was wiser than any general who, in my mind at that time, were the wisest of all."

Hearing Papa speak so openly about his feelings toward her mother brought a warmth of embarrassment to Fernanda's face. But it made her feel closer to him, and to Mama.

"Your mother lived with other Pimas at the Caborca mission," Papa continued. "The Pimas called her Heosig—Flower—for the blossom-shaped birthmark on her cheek. As you know, her parents were killed by Apaches, although she was too young to remember the circumstances of their deaths. The priests raised her with other orphaned children."

Poor Mama, Fernanda thought and shivered despite the warm evening. Wanting to speak of happier things, she asked, "How did you and Mama come to marry, Papa?"

"I knew how the missions operated, structures put into place by the Jesuits. When boys and girls reached a certain age, marriage was arranged by the *madores,* the children's supervisors." Papa drew on his cigarro and blew smoke out into the night. "Understand, Mi'ja. Most of the Indians at the mission had a strong Christian faith, including your mother. I believe they had little opportunity to practice their Pima traditions." He ground the burning tobacco into the dirt. "Religion was the one thing my Pima princess—" he closed his eyes briefly, took a deep breath, and then said quietly, "—Pima princess, that's what your mother was to me." After a pause, he continued, "Your mother and I agreed on most things, but not religion."

"Why, Papa?"

Her father hesitated. "There were rumors about the… the ploys the missionaries used to convert the Indians that angered me. And made me lose my faith. Your mother would have obeyed the priests and married the man they'd chosen, even though I knew she loved me. I was very determined, so I hid my displeasure. The priests assumed I was still a Catholic and they seemed to trust me, so they allowed her to marry me. When I retired from the military, the authorities granted me this piece of land, and I brought her here. We lived a beautiful life together."

After a moment, Papa cleared his throat. "Mi'ja."

"Yes, Papa?"

He coughed. "I understood from your mother…that is, she mentioned that you and Nicolas were to marry soon, before the expedition departed."

Poor Papa. He sounded so uncomfortable.

"That's true, but now…" Fernanda said.

"Yes, now." Papa hung his head, and then held Fernanda's hand between his two rough palms. "Mi'ja, I must ask something of you, and Nicolas. A young bride should devote herself to her husband. But I'll need help on the expedition, especially with Ignacio. It will be a hard transition for him, making this journey without his mother. Can the two of you hold off on your marriage until we reach California? Once we are there, you, and all of us, can start fresh."

"Of course, Papa. Of course. I'll talk to Nicolas. I'm sure he'll agree."

So, she had gotten what she had wished for, but at a terrible cost. Her shoulders slumped with the sadness of it all. She missed Mama so much a sharp ache in her chest cut off her breath for a moment.

"I know so little about Mama's past," she said. "Many times she told me I was like her grandmother, but she never explained. Do you know what she meant?"

"When your mother married me, she cut all ties with the Pimas. Finally, one day, she said she wanted to tell me about a confusing and hurtful time in her childhood, but made me promise to never speak of it again. I believe she wanted to relieve herself of the pain and then leave the past behind.

"After her parents died, the priests kept her at the mission rather than returning her to the Pima village. But they allowed her grandmother, Suhna, to visit her. She had a loving relationship with Suhna, and what she loved in her, she must have seen in you, Mi'ja.

"But there came a time when her grandmother stopped visiting, and your mother kept that hurt to herself. When she grew older, she asked the priests what had become of her grandmother. The Jesuits told your mother that Suhna had stolen her away in the dead of night and abandoned her in the desert. The priests found her and brought her back to the mission."

"Abandoned her!" Fernanda imagined her mother's shock at hearing those words. "Why would Great-grandmother do such a thing if she and Mama loved each other?"

"There is no good answer. Even though your mother didn't remember, she thought it must be true since Suhna stopped visiting her."

"How sad Mama and Great-grandmother lost their love for each other."

Papa put his arm around Fernanda and held her close. "These things happen in families, and, unfortunately, they're sometimes never resolved."

Fernanda bowed her head, hiding fresh tears from Papa. She couldn't bear to tell him how angry she'd been with Mama, or how she'd let Mama walk away with their argument unsettled. If only she could go back to that last morning when Mama had praised her cooking, had playfully pulled her braid, had reached out to her. Fernanda would abandon her selfish pride and tell Mama she and Nicolas would marry. Oh, to see the bright joy that she was sure would have been on her mother's face. But it was too late. "And…and Mama…never saw Great-grandmother again?"

"Your mother didn't say, and I honored her wish and never spoke of it again. She had her own ways, as you know: few words and little expression. As you also know, behind her calm exterior lay courage, wisdom, and love. That spirit, Mi'ja, *her* spirit, will guide us on the journey to California."

Fernanda looked up at the stars that filled the sky like tossed handfuls of glittering sand. *Mama, I'll make you proud of me. You'll see. Promise you'll watch over us.*

She held her father's hand as they watched the moon rise. Thinking of her great-grandmother, Fernanda wondered if she had truly been as wild as Mama said. Mama had likened Fernanda to her, and she felt some kinship, some link to her great-grandmother. She didn't believe the priests' story. *As surely as her blood flows in my veins, I know she loved you, Mama, and she wouldn't have left you. Something else must have happened.*

The pain of her own unresolved fight with her mother wrenched her stomach. Somehow, she'd make it up to Mama. On the journey, she'd find out more about Mama and her peo-ple, *Fernanda's* people. She'd ask every Pima she met about Heosig and Suhna. She'd learn the truth, and the truth would be a gift to Mama. A gift, but also an offering of the love she should have shown her mother the day she died.

Part Two:

The Journey

Mission San Gabriel
Colorado
Gila
Salt
River
Casa Grande
Colorado Crossing
Gila
River
Santa Cruz
San Xavier
del Bac
Tubac Presidio
Baja California
Sonora
Horcasitas

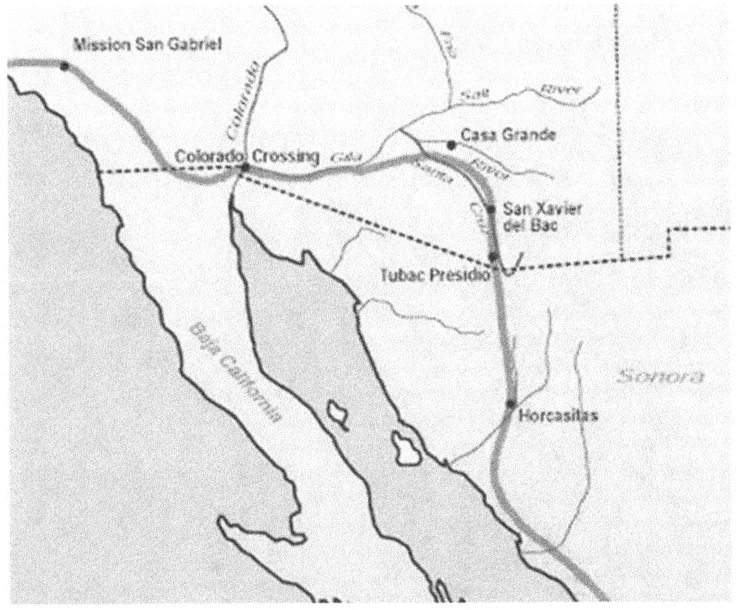

 Chapter Five

October 23, 1775

Everybody mount," Captain Anza commanded, "and our journey will begin."

Fernanda lifted Ignacio onto her mule while eyeing Luis's horse. *Not fair!* she shouted to herself for the hundredth time. Because of the Apache raid, many people had to settle for mules, and the younger children shared mounts with adults or, like Antonio and Marcos, with each other. Papa, of course, deserved a horse, but why should Luis get one and not she? Raising her chin, she stroked her mule's muzzle. "You'll get me to California as well as any silly horse, *mi amiga.* Yes, we'll fly to California. I'll name you Aletta, Winged One."

She climbed up behind Ignacio, flicked the reins, and Aletta, along with the rest of the procession, marched forward. Dust and the smell of manure rose in the air. Cows mooed, bells clanged, children wailed. Vaqueros trotted their whinnying horses around the cattle, horses, and pack mules, their shouts and whips chasing any strays back into the herd.

The pack mules brayed, complaining about their loads: tents, food, shovels, iron pans, the colonists' saddlebags and trunks. Earlier, Fernanda had packed the family's blankets and clothes into a trunk, including wool petticoats for her, and wool gloves and cloaks for the entire family, which Captain Anza had also supplied. She couldn't imagine the need for such heavy clothes.

She'd also brought Mama's special silk rebozo beautifully embroidered with butterflies, though now worn and frayed. On top of her mother's shawl lay Fernanda's new petticoat, skirt, blouse, and rebozo, safe and clean until her arrival in California. Today, though, she wore the new red ribbon in honor of the journey's beginning.

Nicolas rode up to the Marquina family. Even though most everyone's faces were beaded with sweat, his was barely damp. "So, we begin our journey." His voice and eyes were bright with excitement. Under his leather vest, he wore a new blue military coat with red cuffs and collar.

"How far will we travel today?" Papa asked.

"The first camp is five leagues north of Tubac at La Canoa." Nicolas glanced at the sun. "It's nearly eleven o'clock now. We should reach camp by three."

"We stop so soon?" Fernanda asked, thinking she could run all the way to California.

"Believe me," Nicolas said, "when we reach La Canoa, you'll be ready to rest."

Ramona trotted up on a chestnut horse.

A horse! Fernanda fumed, her breath trapped in her chest.

Ramona wore all the new finery provided by the captain: a blue ribbon wove through her long braid, a crisp white petticoat peeked out from a skirt hemmed in lace, and a blue-and-white-striped rebozo slipped below her shoulders.

Fernanda's chest tightened even more, and she pulled her braid, tied with the shiny new ribbon, over her shoulder.

"Buenos dias, Señor Marquina," Ramona said to Papa, sounding as polite as could be, but eyeing Nicolas the entire time.

"I see you were assigned a horse," Fernanda said.

"Yes, my father arranged it. He has some influence with the military, isn't that right, Nicolas?" She tilted her head and smiled up at him so sweetly Fernanda could almost see the sugar crystals forming on her lips. A douse of cold water would melt that smile, no doubt.

Nicolas cleared his throat, shifted in his saddle, blushing. He was probably used to women's attention, but Ramona was so forward. Couldn't she see he wasn't the least bit interested?

"Your horse looks to be a fine animal," Fernanda said. "But for a long and arduous journey such as this, I think a mule is much more dependable." She gave Aletta a vigorous pat on the mule's side.

"Actually, you're quite right, Fernanda," Nicolas said. "Mules can handle—" Ramona's look of dismay and Fernanda's smug smile stopped him, likely realizing he'd gotten into the middle of the girls' spat.

Papa bowed his head and scratched an eyebrow, obviously attempting to hide his smile.

Ramona tossed her head, said, "Buenos dias," and trotted off.

Nicolas cleared his throat again. "Hey, *muchacho*," he said to Ignacio. "How would you like to ride with me?"

Ignacio bounced. *"Si, si!"*

Fernanda had been staring with burning eyes at Ramona's back, and now she helped her brother crawl over to Nicolas's saddle.

"I'll return him soon," Nicolas said and, looking relieved to be escaping, cantered back to the soldiers.

While the boys chattered with Papa about Captain Anza's sword, his fine horse, and his uniform, Fernanda nudged Aletta, and they drifted off among the other colonists. She imagined herself an experienced horsewoman such as New Spain had never seen. She'd jump Aletta over the crowd and gallop to California all on her own. To Monte Rey—King's Mountain—where surely not mere rocks but gold covered the hillsides, and people dressed in silk with intricate embroidery would greet her and ask her to join their feast of fresh meat, fruit, and chocolate.

A raucous laugh interrupted her daydream, and nearby a woman nodded left then right at two men who rode beside her. "Assuredly," the woman said in a loud throaty voice, "it was a sight you wouldn't have believed." She looked to be in her early twenties. Tied securely in her shawl, and sleeping peacefully against her chest, was an infant. A girl, perhaps four years old, sat in front of the woman, clutching the saddle horn. "Now there's a rival to contend with. What a beauty!"

Fernanda's face grew hot when she realized the woman referred to her.

"Come, *Potra Bonita*," the Señora said. "Tell us your name."

Fernanda grinned at the name Potra Bonita: Pretty Filly. "I'm Fernanda. Fernanda Rosalia Marquina. I'm traveling with my father and five brothers."

"Oh ho! What you must endure with so many men in your household. My name is Feliciana Maria Arballo. Please call me Feliciana. I'm an expert on men I'll have you know. And I'm at your service should you ever need my assistance."

Fernanda laughed. "Thank you, I'll remember that." She glanced at the men riding with Feliciana.

"No, neither of these fine gentlemen is my husband," Feliciana said. "I'm traveling with my two daughters." A look of sorrow seemed to cloud her eyes for a moment. Then a smile cleared the sadness from her eyes, and she gently placed her hand on the little girl's head. "This is Tomása. Say hello, Mi'ja."

"Hola, Señorita," Tomása said with a quiet lisp.

"This is my new little one, Estaquia." Feliciana kissed the baby's head. Then she eyed Fernanda from head to toe. "What beautiful hair and pretty red ribbon. I see you're the practical sort not wearing your new clothes, unlike many of the women here."

Thinking of Ramona, Fernanda decided she quite liked this woman. "Yes, I'm saving them for California. They'll surely be ruined if I wear them now."

"You might risk it at least once on the journey. There could be some occasion, a fandango, perhaps—?"

Others who had drawn their horses nearer murmured excitedly, "Fandango?" "Did she say fandango?"

"Yes, possibly," Feliciana said, though still addressing Fernanda. "A fandango where you might want to look your prettiest to dance with some handsome soldier."

How could they have such a dance while traveling? Even though Fernanda thought the idea sounded impossible, she imagined her new petticoat brushing against her calves as she twirled around Nicolas and the other dancers. "Perhaps," she said. "Now I must return to my family. I enjoyed talking with you, Feliciana, and meeting your darling daughters."

"We'll talk again, Potra. Goodbye." Feliciana turned back to the men who couldn't seem to take their eyes off her.

Fernanda made her way back to Papa, thinking what a brave woman Feliciana was to come on the journey with an infant and young daughter. Had something tragic happened to her husband? Forcing her thoughts away from tragedies and sorrow, she sang Feliciana's nickname in her head, *Potra, a filly is what I am. I'll dance and prance my way to California!*

She noticed a young man and girl who'd been listening to Feliciana, the girl smiling, the man scowling. They rode beautiful horses: strong limbs, shiny coats, and silky manes. They sat on skillfully tooled saddles. Then she realized they were the ones she'd seen riding past her home when the expedition arrived in Tubac. The memory of the young man's look rippled through her body.

Fernanda thought he might be eighteen or nineteen. Even though he appeared to be dressed casually, it was obvious that his clothes were of the highest quality. The majority of men, in spite of the heat, wore either jackets or mantles, capes saved for formal occasions or traveling. This man's scarlet jacket was bundled and tucked into a saddlebag. The finely woven cotton of his blue shirt, free from grime and sweat, settled softly over the breadth of his shoulders and muscled biceps. The collar lay open, exposing small beads of sweat on his broad chest. His weren't the thick, practical plush of most men's breeches Fernanda was used to seeing in Tubac. Instead, though the material looked durable, it was thinner and showed off the thick muscles of his thighs, the same way his stockings clung to his toned calves.

The girl, close to Luis's age, was also richly dressed. She wore a white silk rebozo woven with red flowers and threads of gold and silver. Her skirt, the color of burnished silver, was also silk, and a red ribbon with the same gold and silver embroidery as her shawl decorated the end of her braid.

Why were they on this expedition? Certainly poverty hadn't prompted them to join. Their looks made it clear they were brother and sister. Where were their parents? As Fernanda passed them, the girl smiled shyly at her. Both her and her brother's eyes were dark, though hers were warm and friendly, his hard and hostile. She remembered his eyes from that day in Tubac, eyes that had revealed such compelling, yet fleeting, emotions—shock, anguish…desire?—she couldn't look away. Now, they held only anger.

Fernanda reined Aletta alongside the girl's horse. "What beautiful horses you have," Fernanda said.

"Thank you." The girl seemed guarded, and she glanced at her brother.

"My name is Fernanda. I must confess I know your name: Gloria. Do you remember giving my brother the top the day you first arrived in Tubac?"

Gloria's face brightened. "Yes, I do. What a darling boy he is." Her soothing musical voice reminded Fernanda of the mourning doves that nested near her house in Tubac. "Then you remember my brother, Miguel."

Strands of black hair had escaped his loosely plaited braid, and he raked them from his face with his fingers. Fernanda noticed a scar that ran close to his ear past his jaw and partway down his neck.

"Yes," Fernanda said. She smiled, but then it faltered when he said nothing, his face rigid.

His coldness seemed to flush right through her, and she was embarrassed and angry with herself for thinking his look had had some meaning. She raised her chin, turned from him, and said to Gloria. "You've been traveling since Horcasitas?"

"Yes," Gloria said. "For four weeks now."

"You're experienced then," Fernanda said, winking. "Perhaps we can join forces and camp together. My family would appreciate learning from you and sharing what we can."

"Oh, yes! We—"

Miguel quickly interrupted his sister. "There's no need to share your provisions." His voice was quiet, controlled. All the feeling he held back from his voice escaped through his black eyes. "We will camp by ourselves. I have a responsibility to my sister, and I won't have anyone interfering."

"Miguel, she meant no harm," Gloria said.

Something flashed in his eyes. This time not fury, but, shocked, Fernanda realized it was fear. Though he gazed at her, his mind was obviously elsewhere. His eyes flickered. His lips moved as if he was going to speak. Then his eyes snapped back to their dark temper.

"As I said, we only need each other." His already stern face turned as hard and impenetrable as the rocks scattered across the desert. "That's how we'll survive the journey, as well as our lives in California."

Madre de Dios! Such a rude man. "Your sister is correct, I meant no harm. And sometime you may find you *will* need more than each other, at least for your sister's sake."

"Fernanda." Nicolas rode up with Ignacio perched on his saddle. "I've been looking for you. Ignacio wants to ride with you now." While he spoke, he darted glances at Miguel and Fernanda. "Is there a problem?"

Miguel's mouth twisted as if he might spit at Nicolas. Then he eyed Fernanda pointedly and said, "My sister and I wish to be left alone."

Nicolas waved his hand toward Fernanda. "She can be a little…ah, overly…passionate."

"I did nothing!" How could Nicolas assume she'd acted inappropriately? How could he not put this rude beast in his place? Was he blind to the snarl on Miguel's face?

Nicolas straightened his back. "I don't know what happened here, but it's my duty as a soldier on this expedition to ensure that all goes smoothly."

"You think you can flaunt your authority," Miguel said. "No soldier will tell me what I must do."

"Wha–what?" Nicolas sputtered. "While on this journey you *will* obey—"His eyes narrowed. "You. It *is* you. I'll take no more of your insolence, you—"

"Please hand over Ignacio," Fernanda interrupted. Angry with Nicolas, but startled by Miguel's hatred, she simply wanted to leave. "Papa will be wondering what's become of me." She settled Ignacio in front of her on her saddle and then said to him, "This is the nice girl who gave you the top."

Ignacio's eyes widened in recognition. "Gracias!" he said.

"He plays with it all the time," Fernanda said. "It was a pleasure seeing you."

"I hope to see you again," Gloria said, glancing at Miguel, who sat on his horse as stiff as a bronze statue.

"I'll escort you back to your father," Nicolas said.

"No need," Fernanda said. "I can find my way."

Nicolas set his lips. "I will escort you."

Fernanda shrugged then reined Aletta around and nudged her into a walk. She heard Nicolas say coldly, "Remember my words." She knew he was talking to Miguel, but she heard no response. Nicolas trotted up and rode by her side, but she didn't speak to him as they made their way back to her family.

Fernanda settled into the monotonous clop-clop-clop-clop of Aletta's hooves on the sun-baked ground. Besides slowing the mule's steps, the hot rays seared Fernanda's thoughts and any desire to talk. She covered her and Ignacio's heads with her rebozo, but she didn't know which was worse, the sweltering, steamy heat beneath the shawl or the scorching sun that made Ignacio's hair hot to the touch. Sometimes she let the shawl slip to her shoulders, and she'd blow air onto Ignacio's neck and then lift her braid, hoping for a breeze to cool her sweaty skin.

The sun hung halfway down in the sky when Captain Anza gave the order to halt. Fernanda helped Ignacio down from the mule and then stretched. Glancing over her shoulder, she rubbed her bottom. Nicolas was right. She was happy they weren't going any farther that day.

Luis retrieved their pack mule from the muleteers, and Papa and the boys began setting up the tent. Fernanda grabbed a leather bucket and went in search of water. The camp had been transformed into a makeshift town. Soldiers created shelters by draping their capes and blankets over branches of trees that grew near a small stream. The colonists had raised their tents, and they were lined up in orderly fashion. Servants set up tents for the priests and a large round one for Captain Anza.

Fernanda followed others to a wooden trough that had been built in the middle of a spring so livestock could drink without muddying the water, and she realized the camp, La Canoa, had obviously been named after the canoe-shaped trough. She stepped into the line of colonists waiting to fill their containers. Ramona stood a few people ahead of her, and they glared at each other. Miguel and Gloria walked past, Miguel carrying a bucket filled with water. Fernanda caught him glancing at her, and she raised her chin and deliberately turned from him. She sighed. She was supposed to be making friends, not enemies.

Gloria stopped and said hello, and just as Fernanda was about to speak to her, the cattle, in a cloud of dust, thundered toward the spring. The vaqueros, trying to herd the beasts, shouted, "Step aside. Let them through!"

Fernanda grabbed Gloria's hand. Miguel dropped his bucket, wrapped his arms around each of their shoulders, and forced them out of the cattle's path.

Fernanda stumbled, and Miguel's grip tightened, pulling her close to him. She had clasped his shoulder to stop her fall, and now, with her body pressed against his, she became aware of the soft cotton of his shirt and the firmness and strength of his body. She looked up at him, and for a moment their eyes locked. Miguel had the same look on his face as that day in Tubac. The look that erased his anger. The look that again made her heart skip, her breath catch, her cheeks grow hot. A heat he also must feel beneath the flush that spread across his face.

Gloria whimpered, and Miguel released Fernanda. Hugging his sister, he asked her, "Are you okay?"

"Yes," Gloria said, but her face was a faded dusty brown.

Miguel kept his arm around her and, avoiding Fernanda's eyes, said, "I need to refill the bucket."

Downstream, soldiers dug in the sand to bring more water from the spring. Fernanda pointed toward the soldiers, picked up her bucket, and with Gloria between her and Miguel, they walked to the new watering hole.

Fernanda said to Gloria, "Those animals must have been terribly thirsty. I suppose they wanted to be first in line."

Gloria giggled and the color returned to her skin.

Miguel's face had locked up again, and he didn't react to Fernanda's joke.

Fernanda filled her bucket, and then said, "I must get back to my family." She hugged Gloria and said goodbye without meeting Miguel's eyes. As she walked away, she thought how sweet Gloria was, and how volatile Miguel was, how unpredictable. Her brothers annoyed her to no end, but at least she knew what to expect. Miguel, though…

She glanced over her shoulder for one last look.

Miguel was smiling down at his sister.

Huh! Fernanda hadn't known he was capable of smiling. But she dropped her derision when he smoothed Gloria's hair and spoke in a gentle manner. He refilled their bucket and took her hand. As he led Gloria away, he kissed the top of her head.

Fernanda slowly walked back to camp. She would never have believed Miguel was capable of such affection. Something else lay hidden behind his anger, secrets and layers Fernanda would probably never penetrate. Nor did she wish to. But that wouldn't stop her from speaking to Gloria. She clearly wanted a friend. And, as the only girl in each of their families, couldn't they both use a sister?

Chapter Six

October 24, 1775

An old woman sits cross-legged high on a mountain peak, beckoning to Fernanda. The woman's white hair streams from her head, covering the mountain like snow. At the foot of the mountain, Fernanda's mother washes clothes in a stream. Her lips move silently, but Fernanda knows her words: Come, Mi'ja. There's much work to be done.

A girl appears, helping Mama with the laundry. They laugh together. Fernanda turns away and trudges up the mountain, slipping on the snowy hair. A man stands above her and stretches his hand toward her. She can't see his face, but she can hear the gentleness in his voice. "Take my hand," he says. Nicolas, clutching his horse's reins, gallops toward them. His face is angry, and he raises his sword. Fernanda tries to shout, "No!" but the word will not come forth. Nicolas swings his sword. The faceless man slowly topples from the mountain, feet over head over feet, until he splashes into the river. Mama jumps in to save him but the river carries them both away. Mama reaches back, calling in her silent way: Fernanda! Fernanda!

Fernanda woke, her heart racing, tears trickling down her temples. The dream was fading quickly, but Mama had been there…in the river…drowning. She held back a sob so she wouldn't wake Ignacio. She'd seen others, too. An old woman who, in Fernanda's dreamy state, she believed to be her great-grandmother. And Nicolas, striking someone with his sword. She shivered and snuggled closer to Ignacio who kicked his legs then fell back to sleep.

Just as she drifted off, she was startled awake by a woman's cries of pain, and, fainter, the sound of singing. Fernanda sat up. Papa's bedroll was empty. She grabbed her rebozo and crept outside.

All was dark except one tent. The light inside cast over-sized shadows on the canvas. Two figures moved about, and another person appeared to be lying down. Moans and wails escaped the tent. Fernanda tiptoed across the camp. Here and there, eyes peered out of tent openings. Unseen mouths murmured. Papa and another man squatted outside the lighted tent, smoking.

"Papa," she whispered. "What's happening?"

The other man's eyes darted toward the opening of the tent, and he took a long draw on the cigarro clamped between his frowning lips. His face was as gray as the smoke he blew out in nervous puffs.

"Señora Feliz is delivering her baby." Papa leaned close to Fernanda's ear and whispered, "She's having a difficult time."

Fernanda gripped her braid that hung over her shoulder and then cocked her head in the direction of the singing. "Who's singing?"

Señor Feliz said, "Señora Arballo is watching my children." He crushed the cigarro into the ground.

Fernanda squatted next to the men and rolled another cigarette for the distraught father. "How many children do you have, Señor Feliz?"

"Six." The word came out in a raspy croak. He coughed and, nodding toward the tent, said, "And soon, God willing, seven."

Fernanda handed the cigarro to the Señor and stood. "I'll see if I can help Señora Arballo."

She followed the sound of the singing and found Feliciana's tent. Inside, Feliciana sat in the center surrounded by children. Estaquia snuggled against her breast. Tomása and another young one lay with their heads on her lap. She lifted her hand in a small wave to Fernanda, but continued with her song.

> "The baby chicks are saying
> Peep, peep, peep
> It means they're cold and hungry
> It means they need some sleep
> The mother hen finds corn
> She also finds some wheat
> She gathers them together
> And makes sure that they eat
> Mama rocks them in her wings
> And gives her chicks a hug
> All through the night she covers them
> And keeps them warm and snug."

When the song ended, a girl whimpered. Fernanda took her in her arms and rocked her.

Feliciana whispered, "Any news of Manuela Feliz?"

One boy and his sister watched Fernanda with wide eyes. She shook her head slightly at Feliciana, and then winked at the children. "You should have a new brother or sister soon. For now, we should try to get some sleep. Perhaps Feliciana will lull us to sleep with one last song."

As Feliciana began to sing, Fernanda lay down on a bedroll. The brother and sister snuggled into their blankets. Fernanda smoothed the head of one child and gently rubbed another's back. She closed her eyes, and the words of the lullaby mingled with her thoughts.

"Go to sleep, my baby
Sleep in peace and dream."

...poor children...they need their mother...she'll be fine...

"For when you awaken..."

Mama...you were in my dream tonight. And Great-grandmother was there, too. How do I know it was her?

"I will give you cream."

I do...I just do...

Fernanda woke and blinked in the darkness. The children and Feliciana were breathing evenly. Fernanda tiptoed from the tent into a light drizzle and covered her head with her rebozo. She found her father asleep on the ground outside the Feliz's tent. Someone had draped a soldier's cape over him. Gently shaking his shoulder, she whispered, "Papa, Papa."

Her father woke, rubbed his face, and sat up.

"Papa, how are Señora Feliz and the baby?"

He held Fernanda's hand. "Señor Feliz has a healthy baby boy. But his wife didn't survive."

An icy chill washed over Fernanda. She swayed. *Didn't survive…*

Papa jumped up and held her arms. "Mi'ja, sit down. I'm sorry, I should have prepared you."

"N–no, Papa, I'm fine." But she leaned against her father, her head dizzy. *Will I never forget that day…the river… Mama's face…?*

"Is Señora Arballo still with the Feliz children?" Papa asked. "Perhaps you should return to them. Señor Feliz will be there shortly."

She glanced toward Feliciana's tent, knowing the older woman could use her help. But she was so sick of death and sorrow. She'd done her share. "Papa, I–I'm worried about Ignacio. He may be awake and wondering where we are. Surely one of the other women will help Feliciana."

Papa kissed her forehead. "It's been a difficult night, Mi'ja. Yes, return to our tent and comfort Ignacio."

Clutching the rebozo beneath her chin, Fernanda trudged back to the tent. She should be helping those children, but she couldn't face it. She crawled into the tent and lay down next to Ignacio who still slept soundly. She stared off into the darkness for some time, and finally slept. But nightmares— Mama tripping in the river, hitting her head, blood and hair flowing downstream…Señora Feliz pushing her baby into the world, grimacing with pain, blood and the baby spilling onto the cot…the Feliz children, Ignacio, the Rábanos, all crying, searching for their mothers—kept her tossing and turning the rest of the night.

Later that morning, she awoke and went to fill her water pouch for the day's travels. The camp was buzzing with news of the birth and death. Fernanda learned Father Garces would travel ahead to the mission at San Xavier del Bac and bury Señora Feliz; because of the heat, the burial had to happen quickly. The colonists would join him a few days later. On the way back to her tent, she saw Feliciana and another woman preparing the Feliz children for the trek to the mission. Fernanda tried to sneak past them, but Feliciana called to her.

"Where did you disappear to last night?"

Fernanda hesitated, and then walked over to them. "I had to check on Ignacio, and I must have fallen asleep. I–I'm sorry."

"This is Señora Gonzales," Feliciana said as she washed a child's tear-streaked face. "We're cleaning these children to make them sparkling and beautiful for their papa, aren't we, little one?" The girl Feliciana washed nodded, her eyes downcast. But she giggled when Feliciana gently tweaked her nose.

"And then a delicious breakfast," Señora Gonzales said. She patted one boy's rump and reached for the next child.

Fernanda had been backing away, hoping to return to her tent. But the women's kindness toward the children stopped her. "Perhaps while you wash the children," she said, "I can make their breakfast."

"That would be helpful, Potra." Feliciana touched Fernanda's arm and said quietly, "You, more than Micaela or I, understand how these children feel. You can help them cope with this tragedy."

Fernanda hesitated then said, "I'll be right back." She ran to her tent and returned with a piece of their precious chocolate. She made the camper's atole of powdered cornmeal combined with water and shaved chocolate into it. The younger children's dull eyes brightened as they gulped the drink and licked the chocolate from their lips. The older brother and sister sipped their atole, but their eyes brimmed with tears, and they stopped drinking. The younger ones, seeing their siblings, also began to cry. Fernanda's throat tightened as she fought her own tears. What could she say to them when her own heart was full of such sorrow?

Micaela said brightly, "Come now. Will you waste the delicious chocolate Fernanda has brought you?"

Although Micaela meant well, Fernanda knew others' false happiness hadn't consoled her or her brothers when Mama died, so she doubted it would these children. She put her arms around two of them. "Pobrecitos, you miss your mama, I know. She's in Heaven now, a glorious place where she's so very happy and gets to eat all the chocolate she wants."

Mama, are you happy? Do you drink as much cocoa as you want?

The younger children sniffled and looked at her with interest.

"Yes, chocolate for breakfast, lunch, and dinner," Fernanda continued. "But believe me, she hasn't forgotten you. She's watching you every minute, each of you, with pride and love."

Mama, are you watching me, and Ignacio, the Rábanos, and Luis? Are you watching over Papa?

Fernanda picked up the hands of the oldest Feliz girl. "What is your name?"

"Loreta," the girl said, keeping her head bowed.

"You see, Loreta," Fernanda said. "My–my mama… she–she's also in Heaven, and I miss her so much." Tears blurred her vision. "But she's keeping an eye on my brothers and me and loves us just as if she were sitting here next to me. Perhaps our mothers are right now sharing cocoa, telling each other about their wonderful children. Isn't–isn't that true, Feliciana?"

Feliciana said quietly, "Yes, Potra, that is indeed true."

Loreta gazed at Fernanda, her face still wet with tears. "Thank you for the chocolate, Señorita."

The other children murmured, "Gracias, Señorita."

Loreta helped the youngest child drink his atole. "Antonia," she said, "Doroteo, everyone, we must finish our breakfast. Papa is waiting."

A few days later, at the San Xavier del Bac mission, the newborn was christened Luis Antonio Capistrano Feliz. He wore a white baptismal gown one of the women had fashioned from Señora Feliz's new petticoat. *How beautiful he looks*, Fernanda thought. His mother would have loved this moment. But from her death had come this new life, and surely some part of Señora Feliz's soul had found a home in her baby's heart.

Chapter Seven

October 25-31, 1775

As Fernanda packed the trunk for the day's travels, Nicolas came by and whispered, "Come with me, just for a moment."

"Not now, Nicolas. I must help my father break camp."

"I insist." He grabbed her hand and pulled her away from the other colonists. "It seems I've barely spoken with you since the journey began."

She practically had to trot to keep up as he led her behind the herd of cattle and horses. She hopped over a pile of horse manure.

"Nicolas, I—"

"Shhh." He stopped and held her hands. "Just let me look at you before I return to my duties." He gripped her arms. "These past days have been difficult, I know, and the rest of the journey won't be easy. But once we're in California that will change. Of course, I'll still have to go off on occasional campaigns, but you'll be protected by other soldiers."

Did he only think about soldiers, campaigns, and duties? Was this why he rushed her over here, herding her as if he were a *vaquero* and she a stray cow? She stepped away from the manure, the smell burning her nostrils, and bumped Nicolas's arm. He obviously took this as a signal, and moved closer to Fernanda.

"So beautiful," he murmured, trailing a slow look from her eyes, her lips, down her body, and then back to her lips, where his gaze lingered.

He leaned closer, and she knew he meant to kiss her. Never before had he even tried. Being away from the formalities of everyday life must have emboldened him. If she were a proper lady, she'd push him away. But she had always been curious what it would be like to be kissed…

He whispered her name, pulled her close, and pressed his lips against hers. He moaned, and she wanted to feel his pleasure, her own desire, but she could only think how dry the kiss was, not soft and sweet as she had always imagined. And shouldn't her knees feel weak? Shouldn't the earth tremble beneath her feet?

Nicolas stepped back. "Fernanda, forgive me. I didn't mean to take advantage."

"Nicolas, I'm fine. But I–I truly must go and help Papa." She hurried back to her tent, thinking she should be excited, that she should be floating with the thrill of finally being kissed. But a weight of disappointment anchored her to the earth. She touched her lips and couldn't help thinking, *Is that all there is to a kiss? Is that what all the fuss is about?* Then she threw back her head and laughed. Oh, if only there were someone she could tell that the witnesses to her first kiss were mooing cows, snorting horses, and complaining pack mules.

Later, as the colonists left the mission, Nicolas rode alongside Fernanda, darting glances at her. "Again, I hope you will forgive me."

"Nicolas, there's nothing to forgive." What did he expect her to say?

He sat straighter in his saddle, a proud, proprietary look on his face.

Perhaps I shouldn't forgive him, Fernanda thought. *Not for a kiss such as the one he gave me!* She turned her head away, wanting to laugh, wishing again she had a woman friend to share the laughter with. She caught Ramona watching her conversation with Nicolas. Several horses separated her and Nicolas from Ramona. She always seemed to be wherever Nicolas was, most likely waiting for the opportunity to dig her talons in and carry him off.

Sliding a glance at Ramona's jealous face, Fernanda reached out and touched Nicolas's arm. "How far will we travel today?"

"Probably about six leagues," Nicolas said. "Our destination on this leg of the journey is the Gila River, thirty-two leagues from here, a five or six day march." He addressed the colonists who rode nearby. "Today we leave familiar territory. We won't see Spaniards, missions, or presidios again until we reach California."

Hearing this, Fernanda forgot Ramona. *We're truly leaving our old life behind. What will I see? Who will I meet?*

As if hearing her thoughts, Nicolas swept his arm forward. "Ahead lie deserts and mountains occupied only by Indians."

"Indians?" Antonio asked. "Do you mean Apaches?"

Nicolas was looking off into the distance, and he nodded distractedly. "Captain Anza is conferring with some other soldiers. I'll be back." He trotted away.

All who had heard Antonio's question and seen Nicolas's nod began to chatter and nervously check over their shoulders.

Fernanda's mother had warned them constantly about Apaches, and she had learned to fear them. But stronger than that fear was her excitement at the possibility of meeting the Pimas. Gazing into the expanse of desert before her, she hoped it would be soon.

Along with the other colonists, Fernanda and her family settled into a routine as they made their way to the Gila River. Each morning, everyone congregated outside Father Font's tent, and he said Mass while Fernanda daydreamed and her brothers fidgeted. Because Papa had no religious faith, they'd rarely gone to church in Tubac. Still, at Mama's insistence, the children had been baptized.

After Mass and a breakfast of atole, they would break camp, pack the mules, and walk five or six leagues. When they reached the next camp, they set up their tent and ate dinner, usually beans and tortillas along with dried meat or, occasionally, beef from a slaughtered cow.

Once, as the family sat for their meal, Nicolas surprised them with sausages and cheese.

The boys were ecstatic.

"Beans and rice. Beans and rice," Antonio said. "That's all Fernanda knows how to cook."

"Not to mention the crumbliest crackliest tortillas ever," Marcos said.

"Not like Mama's," Jorge mumbled.

Fernanda fumed. They were so cruel!

"It's food, muchachos," Papa said. "Be thankful for it."

Marcos stabbed a sausage with his fork and asked Nicolas, "Where did you get these?"

Nicolas winked. "That's my secret."

"From the captain," Antonio whispered. "I've seen his servant preparing his meal, and he has the most glorious food. Sausages like these and fresh biscuits and I smelled cinnamon and cloves."

"That's not fair," Jorge said.

Luis defended the captain. "He's the leader of the expedition and has a right to better rations. Isn't that right, Nicolas?"

"Yes," Nicolas said. "Consider these extra provisions a treat, and something to keep to ourselves."

As he left them to their meal, Fernanda ran to him. "Thank you, Nicolas. You won't be reprimanded for giving us the food, will you?"

"No, as long as no one finds out. I'll do what I can to make the journey easier for your family, and for you, Fernanda." He picked up her hand and glanced at her mouth. "I wish we had more moments alone."

Heat rushed to her face.

"Nanda," Jorge called. "Antonio is stealing your share of the sausage."

Nicolas laughed. "You'd better get back to dinner."

"Yes, thank you again."

As she ate, she thought of Nicolas's look and his desire to be alone with her. Losing interest in the sausage, she pushed her plate toward the boys, and they dove for the meat.

Since Nicolas's kiss, she wondered even more about love. She'd enjoyed the physical contact, the feel of Nicolas's arms around her, the adoring look in his eyes, the anticipation of being kissed. She'd been so disappointed with the kiss, though, and, more importantly, that she hadn't felt any strong yearnings of love. She loved him, didn't she? Of course she did. Perhaps she should let him kiss her a second time. Perhaps she didn't have a chance to consider her other feelings because she'd been so surprised by his kiss. He was truly handsome, after all. She sighed and ate the last bite of cheese wrapped in a piece of tortilla.

The land they traveled across was as flat and dry as Fernanda's tortillas. The animals raised clouds of dirt, covering everything with a white dust as fine as flour. Fernanda found the dust in every seam of her clothes, in her food, in her bedding. It matted her hair, irritated her eyes, and coated her teeth. How she longed for a bath, but it would be days before they reached the river.

Ahead, all that broke the straight-lined horizon were scrubby mesquite and *hediondilla*—the little stinker.

"Don't eat those smelly flowers or tough leaves, Aletta. They'll burn your mouth." She patted the mule. "Soon, you'll have plenty to drink and delicious sweet grass."

There was no sign of Apaches or other Indians. When would she see the Pimas? And when she did, how would she talk to them, ask them if they knew of Heosig, her mother, or Suhna, her great-grandmother?

On the morning of the sixth day after leaving the mission, Captain Anza announced they would reach the Gila River that afternoon. As they neared the river, Fernanda was sure she could smell the water. She'd bathe and wash her clothes. No more dust!

She and Luis trotted up toward the front of the train, leaving Papa and the other boys farther back in the long caravan of colonists. Nicolas and the priests also rode in front, behind Captain Anza. They went another league or two, and as the sun touched the desert horizon, a buzz of excitement flew through the crowd.

Luis pointed forward. "Fernanda, look!"

Several Indian men on horseback were cantering toward the procession. One rode slightly ahead of the others and raised his hand in greeting.

Captain Anza returned the gesture, and called to the colonists, "Halt!"

The Indians reined in their horses in front of the captain. Fernanda saw her own fear and excitement mirrored in Luis's wide yes, but not the embarrassment that warmed her cheeks. She'd had contact with Indians at the Tubac presidio, at the market and chapel. But this was the closest she'd been to a "heathen" Indian, as the priests called the un-Christianized Indians. And the Tubac Indians had never been so...so... undressed. These men wore loincloths and roughly cut deerskins wrapped around their waists that barely covered them, if at all. Open-toed moccasins—some ankle-high, others up to their knees—protected their feet. Feathers, flowers, and twigs decorated some of the men's flowing dark hair. Bows and long leather pouches full of arrows were slung across their bare chests. A few carried wooden clubs and rawhide shields.

At the sight of the weapons, Fernanda shifted back in her saddle. Were these Apaches? Nicolas sidled his horse next to hers and said quietly, "Don't be alarmed. These are friendly people. On the last expedition, Captain Anza forged friendships with Indian tribes in this area."

The Indian leader greeted the captain, and an interpreter translated his words. "He says he is chief of the Sutaquison people, a tribe of the Pimas. He and his people welcome you."

Fernanda caught her breath. There were many Pima villages her mother could have come from. Still her chest filled with hope. She must find a way to speak with them.

Off to her right she saw Miguel and Gloria guiding their horses close to Captain Anza and the Pimas. As the Pima leader spoke, Miguel watched him intently as if he understood what the Pima was saying.

Then her mouth dried when the Pima leader handed Anza two scalps.

"Apache," the interpreter said. "Since they're also your enemy, he asks if you're here to help defeat them."

"We won't be engaging in warfare," Captain Anza said, and then explained the reason for the journey. A muleteer brought a mule to the captain. He reached into the saddlebag, pulled out a pouch of tobacco and a fistful of colored glass beads, and handed them to the Pima leader.

The Pima accepted the gifts, and then spoke while pointing behind him.

"He says they'll escort us to our camp," the interpreter explained.

Captain Anza called to the colonists, "We will camp at the lagoon. Tomorrow will be a day of rest."

The crowd cheered. They had pushed forward through the heat and dust to reach the Gila River, and after that day's twelve-league march—double what they usually traveled—they were ready for a break. Fernanda and Luis rode with the priests as the Pimas and Captain Anza led them to the lagoon. Nicolas rode next to Anza, conferring with him.

Fernanda glanced back at Miguel. They're eyes met, and each quickly looked away. Fernanda felt her cheeks flush. She raised her chin, turned again, and waved to Gloria, all the while her heart tapping in her chest.

Surprised at herself, and wishing her heart would stop its ridiculous thumping, she gazed across the desert. A short distance away, she noticed some ruins, and pointed. "What could that be?"

Father Font put his hand to his brow and said in a high-pitched voice, "The Casa Grande! Moctezuma, the great

Aztec leader, built the palace over five-hundred years ago." To the other priests he said, "We must investigate the ruins tomorrow."

Fernanda whispered to Luis, "Wouldn't it be exciting to explore the Casa Grande?" Then she said, "Father, may my brother and I ride with you when you go to the ruins? We won't be a bother, and we'd love to see them."

Luis's eyes lit up. "Yes, please, Father. We're practiced riders and we won't slow you down."

"No," Father Font said. "It's not a pleasure excursion. We want to record the layout of the ruins and take measurements. We can't have children interfering with our work."

Fernanda flounced in her saddle. Huh! Children? Interfere? They merely wanted to look around. She eyed the ruins. Another plan formed in her mind, and it was something far more interesting than riding out with the priests.

At the camp, Fernanda scratched her dirty head, realizing it was too late to bathe. Tomorrow, as soon as she rose, she'd head for the river. She convinced Papa to set up their tent next to Señor Feliz's and Feliciana's, who was nursing the Feliz newborn along with her own Estaquia. Señor Gonzales, his wife Micaela, and their four children also joined the group. They arranged their tents in a circle and shared a fire and dinner. Each night, Señor Gonzales strummed his guitar, and he was teaching Fernanda to play. She had always loved music, but hadn't inherited her mother's beautiful voice. Now she could express the joy music gave her through the guitar.

Other families were forming similar communities. Fernanda noticed Miguel had assembled his tent away from the others. When she saw Gloria looking in her direction, she approached them.

"Please join our little group." She spoke directly to Miguel. "It makes it easier to share. I know my family is happier since Feliciana has helped me with the cooking."

Gloria giggled, but Miguel stared into their fire. "We're fine where we are," he said.

Gloria, looking at Fernanda, nodded discretely toward her brother, her expression obviously apologizing for her brother. "Oh, Miguel," Gloria said. "Wouldn't it be fun to camp with the others?"

To Fernanda, Miguel said, "I'm capable of taking care of my sister."

Whatever it was that had passed between them earlier was gone. Perhaps she had imagined the entire thing. She was a fool.

"I have no doubt you take good care of Gloria," she said. "I was simply trying to be friendly. Can you possibly believe that?"

Miguel said through a tight mouth, "We'll stay here." He picked up a stick and fiercely poked it into the coals of the fire. Sparks exploded into the air and flew toward him and Gloria. Miguel leaped up, pulled Gloria away from the fire, and frantically brushed her skirt.

Gloria grabbed his hand, stopping him. "Miguel," she said quietly. "I'm fine."

A look of helplessness flashed across his face, and his strong body seemed to deflate as he settled again next to the fire. But just as Fernanda was feeling a bit sorry for him, he raised insolent eyes to hers, as if challenging her to make a comment about the fire, or Gloria, or the glimpse she'd seen through the crack in his hardened shell.

Fernanda's arms stiffened at her sides, and she clenched a handful of skirt in each hand. She'd continue her friendship with Gloria, but why let Miguel's unpredictable behavior bother her? "Do as you wish. But you're welcome anytime should you change your mind." She touched Gloria's shoulder and said, "Good night."

As she turned away, the interpreter walked by, and she called out to him, "Señor! *Por favor.* Would it be possible for you to translate for me? I'd like to ask the Pimas some questions."

The interpreter scowled. "Questions? What kinds of questions?"

"Nothing bothersome or unfriendly." She glanced over her shoulder and caught Miguel listening. His eyes darted away. She lowered her voice. "My–my mother was Pima. I just want to know, I want to find out…some things."

"Your mother? Pima? I don't know what you're talking about." And he stalked away.

Fernanda froze momentarily at the interpreter's rudeness, and then glared at his back. She'd find another way to speak to the Pimas. She glanced back at Miguel, who again had been watching her. She felt the heat of humiliation rush to her face. And then the embarrassment was replaced by anger. Madre de Dios! Had he decided to spy on her now? She gave him the same squinty-eyed look she'd given the interpreter, and then marched back to camp.

That evening, as Papa and the Rábanos crawled inside the tent ready for sleep, Fernanda pulled Luis aside. "Let's go to the ruins tonight!"

"Tonight?"

"The moon's full to help us find our way. Of course, Casa Grande must be a few leagues away. We'll have to take horses."

"How can we take horses? The muleteers won't allow us."

"When we unloaded today, I made sure your horse and Papa's were at the outskirts of the pack. Everyone will sleep soundly after today's long march, including the muleteers. Besides, they won't notice two horses are gone, and we'll be back before they're missed."

Luis frowned and slowly shook his head. Before he could speak, she clutched his arm.

"An adventure, Luis, come. Aren't you tired of so much unhappiness? Let's have some fun."

He hesitated then grinned. "All right. We must make sure Papa and the boys are asleep before we go."

"Of course."

Later, Fernanda lay on her bedroll, and though her legs were stiff, her inner thighs chafed, and her bottom sore, she couldn't wait to climb onto Papa's horse. Her brothers and Papa coughed, burped, passed gas—everything, it seemed, except sleep. Oh, the sun would be up before they ever settled down.

Finally, Papa snored, and no other sounds came from the boys. Fernanda was about to sit up when she heard a groan. *Now what?*

Marcos threw off his blanket and crawled out the tent.

I think I just might scream! Fernanda followed him outside and hissed, "Marcos, what are you doing?"

He snorted. "I have to go—" He gestured toward the back of the tent.

Fernanda huffed. "Why didn't you do that earlier?"

Marcos shook his head in disgust and walked around the tent.

Luis crawled out and whispered, "What's going on?

"Marcos." She tossed her head in the direction he'd gone. "Now we'll have to wait until *he* falls asleep before we can go."

Marcos walked up behind them. "Go where?"

"Nowhere," Fernanda said. "Now go back to bed."

"I won't until you tell me."

"Shhh." Fernanda pulled them away from the tent. She and Luis eyed each other.

"Well, you can come if you want," Luis said. "We're going to Casa Grande, and we'll need help scaring away the ghosts. Right, Fernanda?"

Fernanda bit the inside of her cheek. "Oh, yes, there will be many ghosts to scare away."

Marcos shivered. "I'm cold and sleepy. I think I'll go back to bed."

"Well, if you're sure," Luis said.

"Don't wake the others," Fernanda said. "We'll return soon, so there's no need for them to know."

Fernanda and Luis tiptoed through the camp, trying to hold back their giggles. They snuck around the rustling animals, careful not to disturb them beyond the occasional moo, whinny, or bray. Quiet guitar strums and cigarette smoke floated above the herd, but no muleteers were in sight. Fernanda nudged Luis and pointed to their horses. He nodded. They scurried past the other animals, keeping low. Fernanda crouched next to Papa's horse, Luis next to his. Papa's horse snorted and shook its head. Fernanda quickly rubbed its side and it quieted. She peered beneath the horse's belly, looking for any sign of muleteers. Nothing. Then Luis jabbed his elbow into her side and jerked his head to the right. A muleteer sat with his back propped against a bedroll and pack, his head tilted to the side. Luis motioned for her to stay, and her muscles tightened as he crawled toward the muleteer.

A few minutes later, he was back. "He's asleep," he whispered. "Snoring louder than Papa."

Fernanda's shoulders relaxed, and she quickly checked the horses' gear. They wore halters and lead ropes. The rest of the tack lay nearby, but she didn't want to risk waking the muleteer by saddling the animals. She and Luis could use the lead ropes like reins and ride bareback.

She grabbed the lead of Papa's horse and, followed by Luis and his horse, crept away from the herd. They walked until the camp was well behind them. Then Fernanda stopped next to a large rock and pulled up her skirt, exposing the trousers she'd convinced Luis to lend her. Her brother rolled his eyes as she tied the skirt in a knot around her hips. She raised her chin at Luis, and then, stepping on the rock, grabbed the horse's mane and pulled herself onto its back. She loved the feeling of freedom the trousers gave her. Why couldn't she wear them every day? Huh! Just imagine the reactions she'd get from the other campers if she appeared in the morning dressed in rebozo, blouse, and breeches.

Luis climbed onto his horse, and they headed in the direction of the ruins. Seeing no sign of anyone following them, they nudged the horses into a trot.

Oh, you are a beauty, my friend, she silently told the horse. *We will fly, fly to the ruins. A midnight adventure for us both, no?*

She grinned at Luis, but he was peering ahead. "Look, Nanda, up there. Two other riders."

Oh God, Apaches! Fernanda strained to see. No…no, not Indians. A small figure sat on one of the horses. And the other…? A cloud that partially shadowed the moon drifted away into the black sky. In the light of the moon that suddenly shined bright upon the desert, Fernanda saw the riders were Gloria and Miguel.

Chapter Eight

October 31, 1775

"Luis, let them get ahead," Fernanda said. Miguel may have decided to have a late-night adventure, too, but she wouldn't let him spoil this for her.

Gloria and Miguel's horses began to canter, growing smaller until they disappeared into the shadow of the Casa Grande. Fernanda signaled to Luis, and they continued at a slow trot.

Occasional clouds skated across the moon's bright surface, its glow lighting the vast desert and the road that led to the ruins. Outlined in the dark silhouette of the Casa Grande were the different levels and worn rectangular shapes of the structure. Although Fernanda knew the ancient building was large, at this distance in the vast desert, it looked small against the endless star-studded sky.

Giant saguaro cactuses, some of them three or four times Fernanda's height, stood across the sands like soldiers frozen in a stiff salute. The far-off hoot of an owl—who-who-who-whoooo, who-who-who-whoooo—broke the silence of the desert. Fernanda couldn't help ducking when bats dipped and swooped high above her, snatching their insect dinners from the air.

Luis laughed. "They'll not harm you, Nanda."

"I know." She tipped back her head. "I'm not afraid of you, bats. Only envious you can fly about so freely at night."

Luis blew a sound of disgust from his mouth.

When they reached the ruins, they looped the horses' lead ropes around a smaller saguaro trunk. Fernanda untied her skirt and the hem dropped, hiding the trousers. She saw no sign of Miguel or Gloria. While hoping she wouldn't see Miguel, she wondered if Gloria was frightened, or if she enjoyed exploring the Casa Grande.

Arching her back, Fernanda peered up at the three-story-high building towering above her. The moonlight cast shadows through the walls' dark openings and accentuated the deep crevices. She ran her hand over the timeworn earth wall, still warm from the day's heat, smooth in some spots, rough and cracked in others. An eeriness grazed her back like the ethereal touch of ghostly fingers. Her neck and arms tingled. Who had lived there and how long ago? Were ancient eyes peering down at her? She shook her shoulders. She was as silly as Marcos with his fear of ghosts. She tiptoed around the corner, and the wall trailed off into the darkness. Following the wall, she found a shadowy doorway. "Luis," she whispered. "This way."

She stepped into the opening. The thick wall created a high but narrow passage. She crept forward. Darkness and cool air engulfed her. She brushed against the wall, shivered, and hugged her arms close to her body. Something scratched in the dirt near her feet. A scorpion? A tarantula? Holding back a scream, she dashed through to the other side.

Luis ran after her and grabbed her shoulders. "Ay!"

Fernanda gasped, and then shook Luis's hands from her shoulders. "Not funny, little brother."

Luis smiled sheepishly and poked her arm. "Sorry, Nanda."

They stood inside a walled compound open to the sparkling sky. Fernanda, spotting a glint in the moonlight, skipped ahead and picked up a broken piece of pottery. She scanned the ground. "Look, there are pieces scattered everywhere."

Luis picked through the shards and held one up. "This must have been some kind of jar."

Other pieces looked like bits of plates and pots, many stained with faded colors and patterns.

Fernanda squatted next to Luis. "They must be hundreds of years old."

"Probably five hundred," a voice said.

Fernanda jumped up and swung around, wincing as she cut her finger on a shard. Miguel, half hidden in the shadows, stood in the doorway. Fernanda clenched her fists and felt blood oozing from her finger. She breathed in, trying to stop the heavy thud of her heart. "Did you wish to scare us? Well, you didn't succeed."

Gloria ran up behind her brother. "Miguel—" She saw Fernanda and Luis and skipped into the compound. "You came, too? We were just about to climb the watchtower. We can all go."

Luis said, "A watchtower! Where?"

"I'll show you." Gloria dashed out of the compound, followed by Luis.

Fernanda hesitated. She didn't want to share her adventure with Miguel, but what could she do? Gloria was so sweet, so excited to see her and Luis.

"I'm sorry," Miguel said. "I didn't mean to frighten you."

"Huh! You didn't frighten me. It's just that I cut my finger on a piece of this pottery." She stepped to the center of the compound where the moon shone brightest. Turning her back to Miguel, she examined her finger. Footsteps crunched behind her then stopped.

"I'm sorry," Miguel said again. "Is your finger okay?"

Fernanda didn't respond, but she relaxed her tight shoulders at Miguel's softened tone, reminding her of his tenderness toward Gloria. She glanced up at him through her downcast lashes, and then back at her finger. He took her hand. His was warm, and she could feel the strength beneath his gentle grasp, the callouses from weeks of riding. It was the roughness of his hands that made her chest flush with heat, that made him suddenly, physically, real, and she couldn't help but wonder what those hands would feel like caressing her cheek, what it would feel like to be embraced by him, kissed by him…

"It–it's a small cut," she said. "The bleeding's stopped."

Miguel untied the kerchief from around his neck and wrapped it around her finger. "This way the wound won't reopen, and it'll stay clean."

Fernanda murmured, "Thank you." She pulled her hand away, and he hesitated briefly before letting go. Fernanda turned from his gaze, heat still pulsing through her body. She gestured at the broken pottery. "Is it truly five-hundred years old?"

Miguel picked up a curved fragment. "Yes. The Hohokam were master craftsmen and used their beautiful pottery for trading."

"The Hohokam? Who were they?"

Miguel flipped the shard back and forth between his hands. "They were farmers, peaceful people. They lived in this region for many centuries. They built this grand house, an entire village actually, five hundred years ago."

"How do you know so much about these people?"

"My—" Pain seemed to flicker briefly on his face. "Someone told me the story of the Hohokam, the grand cities they built, their mysterious disappearance."

"Their mysterious disappearance?"

"No one knows why, but they abandoned their communities. Some believe they dispersed and divided into the two tribes of the Papagos and Pimas, the Desert People and the River People.

"Pimas!" Fernanda said. "My mother's from the Pima tribe."

"Yes, I heard you say so earlier." Miguel's lips twitched in a slight smile. "Who knows? We might be distant cousins. My–my relatives, some of them, are Papagos." He nodded at the doorway. "Should we find Gloria and your brother?"

Fernanda followed Miguel through the dark passage, forgetting about scorpions and tarantulas as she thought how Miguel had lost his nasty scowl, especially when talking about the Pimas and Papagos. He had Papago blood, and seemed to know a lot about them. Perhaps he could help her learn more about the Pimas and even help her speak to them. On the other side of the thick wall, she spotted Gloria and Luis on top of the ruins.

Gloria waved and shouted, "Up here!"

"We're coming," Fernanda called.

Walking toward them, Miguel said, "Your mother…she isn't with you?"

Fernanda's throat tightened. "She–she died a short time ago."

Miguel nodded. "I'm sorry."

"And your parents?" Although Fernanda guessed what the answer must be.

"They, too—" Miguel's voice sounded dry, and he swallowed, "—they too are no longer alive."

"I'm sorry, also." Wishing to lighten the mood, Fernanda said, "It seems we have much in common. My mother rarely spoke of her life before marrying my father. I know little of the Pimas' ways. But my father, he's the proud Spaniard in every way."

"Oh, yes, the proud Spaniard." Fernanda was surprised to see Miguel's scowl had returned. "The excuse the Spaniards always use, especially the soldiers, to mistreat the Indians. Why do you only know of your father's, the Spanish, ways? Why do you know nothing about your mother's people?"

"How dare you say such a thing? You know nothing of my mother *or* my father and our life together." But her anger faltered. What Miguel said went to the core of some of her doubts and regrets; she should have found out more about her mother's life when she had the chance. And it brought back the ache of her last morning with Mama.

She sprinted to join Luis and Gloria. Why did it concern him? He had no right to make her think about those sorrowful things.

Miguel ran ahead, jumped on the wall, and stretched his hand toward Fernanda. His face was hidden in the shadows, his body silhouetted against the white moonlight-sheen of the tower. "I'm sorry," he said, his voice gentle. "I didn't mean to upset you. Here, take my hand."

The back of her neck bristled as if hundreds of cactus spines pricked her skin. It was just like her dream when the faceless man helped her to the top of the snowy mountain. She glanced over her shoulder, half-expecting to see Nicolas charging toward them.

As Miguel pulled her up, she looked into his eyes. Usually as cold and dark as a starless sky, his eyes now held a warmth that softened his face. Whether it was his look or the grasp of his hand, or both, Fernanda didn't know. She caught her breath and stopped for what must have been one second, but could have been minutes or hours or days. She hugged her waist with her other arm, as if an arrow carrying a feeling she didn't understand shot straight through her, spreading its flame into her stomach, her heart, her entire being.

She stood next to him and pulled her hand away. "Thank you," she said, avoiding his eyes. She kicked at the hem of her skirt and murmured, "I can't climb in this." As she tied the skirt around her hips, she realized Miguel would probably be shocked when he saw her trousers. Shocked as any man would be. She lifted her chin, ready to challenge his disapproval.

Instead, he eyed the pants and then gave her an appraising look. Then he nodded slightly, as if confirming some earlier thought. He began to climb the tower, and Fernanda followed. The uneven edges of the tower formed rough steps, and she inched her way up, soon joining Miguel, Luis, and Gloria at the top.

Turning in a circle, Fernanda surveyed the desert and the rest of the ruins. "How glorious to have such a view. Now I'll know, at least a little, how the hawk feels next time I see one soaring high above my head."

Luis snorted, but Miguel gazed at her, again wearing a smile that warmed his eyes—and her face. She untied her skirt. "Look," she said. "The ruins go on in all directions."

Miguel stepped to her side and pointed. "See that large ditch? It leads to the river and must have been an aqueduct that supplied water to the villagers."

Luis said in a hushed voice, "Those giant saguaros look like ancient spirits marching across the desert."

Fernanda laughed. "Now who's afraid of ghosts?"

"The saguaros *are* ghosts," Gloria whispered. "Miguel, tell the cactus story."

"The cactus story?" Fernanda asked.

"It's an old Papago myth of how the saguaros came to this land," Miguel said.

As he stared out across the desert, Fernanda studied his profile. He stood as tall as Nicolas, but appeared larger with his muscular build. Certainly Nicolas was more handsome with his refined Spanish features. Still, Fernanda thought Miguel handsome, too, with the curve of his high cheekbones, his strong jaw and full lips, his broad nose, his skin brown and smooth except for the scar.

Miguel sat down and dangled his legs over the tower's edge. The others did the same.

"Once, long ago," Miguel began, "there came to this country a man called The Drinker. He became angry with the people who lived here, so he devised a plan to destroy them. He would climb a high mountain and send so much water that all the land and all the people would be covered. He told Coyote and Dog of his plan, and they agreed to help. So, The Drinker caused the skies to open, and much water flowed onto the land. Dog informed the angry man when the water covered the land and people, and The Drinker stopped the rain."

Luis scoffed. "A dog that could talk?"

"In those days," Miguel said, "the animals talked."

Luis rolled his eyes; Fernanda nudged him and grinned, and Miguel continued. "After some time, The Drinker told Coyote and Hummingbird to bring him some mud. From this mud, The Drinker formed several men. Some of the men made their village downstream, and some made their village upstream. The people who lived downstream were friendly and spoke a language The Drinker could understand. But he couldn't understand the people who lived upstream. This displeased him. He called these people the Bad Men."

"The Apaches," Luis said.

"Shhh!" Gloria glanced over one shoulder, and then the other. "Please keep your voice down."

"Only the ghosts can get you up here," Luis said. But he also checked behind him.

"Let Miguel finish his story," Fernanda whispered.

Miguel leaned toward the others and lowered his voice. "The Drinker was so unhappy with the Bad Men, he decided he would destroy several of their villages. He lowered the sun in the sky, burning the Bad Men. They begged for mercy, but The Drinker didn't listen. Instead, he transformed them into saguaros." Miguel paused and waved his arm slowly over the desert. "And that's why there are so many saguaros in this country."

They were all silent. Fernanda stared down at the saguaros, and then cocked her head. A lonely lament echoed across the desert, joined by several more howls, and then quick yips.

"Coyotes," Luis said.

"Perhaps The Drinker has returned," Miguel said. Just then, their horses whinnied, and Miguel raised his eyebrows at the others, as if he'd been proven right.

Fernanda folded her arms close to her chest. As she listened to the coyotes' mournful, eerie cries, she couldn't help feeling a little sorry for them and their life of wandering the desert. Thinking of Miguel's story, she asked, "Do you think the bad men in the legend are meant to be Apaches?"

Miguel shrugged. "The Apaches are the enemies of most, including the Pimas, Papagos, Yumas, and the Spaniards. So, most likely, that's who the bad men are meant to be."

"The Apaches are devils," Luis said. "They steal horses and cattle, they burn settlements and murder people."

Miguel snapped his head toward Luis. "The Spanish soldiers aren't any better. They kill the Apache warriors and capture the women and children. Then they keep them as slaves."

"The soldiers are only trying to protect us." Luis clenched his hands into fists. "Besides, Captain Anza demanded we treat the Indians well."

"I can tell you, the soldiers don't always obey." Miguel stood and kicked the ancient stone, sending a shower of crumbling rock down to the desert floor.

"Miguel," Gloria said. Tears brightened her eyes.

Miguel sat next to Gloria and put his arm around her shoulders. "I'm sick of all fighting. I hope to find a peaceful life for my sister and myself in California."

"Nicolas told me I'd make a good soldier," Luis said. "That's what I intend to be."

"If that's how you want to live your life…" Miguel pulled a wooden flute out of his shirt and began to play.

Fernanda lay back and stared at the stars, enjoying the slow high notes of Miguel's flute. What a confusing person he was: kind and gentle one minute, angry and rude the next. Angry, but also "sick of all fighting." She thought of Luis and Miguel's argument. She couldn't blame Mama for teaching her children to hate and fear Apaches, but perhaps it wasn't so one-sided after all.

Why did Luis want to be a soldier? What of her being a soldier's wife? Though Nicolas always stressed (and Mama had, too) the security his soldier's stipend and land grant would give them, what would the reality of their daily life be? She'd only been concerned about the monotony, but what about the fighting? Would she be worrying if her husband had survived the most recent Apache attack and praying her children would be safe?

Fernanda closed her eyes and imagined the notes from Miguel's flute rising above the desert, above the saguaros and coyotes, floating up to the stars with their song of peace…

Fernanda jumped at the sound of shouts and pounding hooves. Luis and Gloria sat up, rubbing their eyes. Miguel was already standing, squinting down at the desert.

Fernanda scrambled to her feet. "What is it? I can't believe we fell asleep!" The sky was still dark, but the air had chilled, and she sensed it was very late. Or very early morning.

"Soldiers from the expedition," Miguel said. "They must be searching for us."

Four soldiers galloped toward the ruins, and as they got closer, Fernanda saw that one of them was Nicolas. He'd be angry. And Papa…

She braced her shoulders as if against a coming attack. "We should let them know we're here." She waved and shouted, "Nicolas!"

Nicolas reined his horse, stopping abruptly. Then he and the other soldiers raced to the base of the tower.

Nicolas shouted up to them, "You have the camp frightened and in an uproar." He clasped the hilt of his sword. Out of habit, Fernanda knew, but he looked angry enough to yank it out of the scabbard and strike something, or someone. "Luckily, Marcos told us you had snuck off to the ruins. Without permission. Come down now!"

Miguel held his fists at his sides. "You have no right to tell us what to do."

Nicolas's mouth dropped open. "I have *every* right." His voice cracked. "As long as you're on this expedition, you're under the orders of Captain Anza. And that means you're under my or any other soldier's orders."

"What will you do if I don't obey your *orders*?" Miguel spat the last word at Nicolas. "What will you do? Kill me?" He helped Gloria down from the ruins and lifted her up to her horse's saddle. Then he leaped onto his horse and edged next to Nicolas. "Well, soldier. Is that what you'll do? Kill me?" Then he did spit—on the ground in front of Nicolas's horse. "Soldier," he said again with so much hate and contempt that from his lips it became a dirty word. He whirled his horse around, said, "Come, Gloria," and they galloped off across the desert.

Nicolas pulled his sword partway from its scabbard and glared at Miguel's retreating figure. Fernanda cringed at the hatred that blazed between the two men. Nicolas did not brandish his sword. Miguel did not topple from the tower. But her dream had come true, at least in part, after all.

Chapter Nine

November 1-2, 1775

Fernanda picked up a piece of dough and formed a tortilla, slapping it between her hands.

Feliciana stood nearby, stoking the fire. "Do those tortillas deserve the punishment you're giving them? Why don't I make them. You can chop this meat and add it to the beans."

Fernanda traded places with Feliciana and said, "I can't stop thinking about Casa Grande."

"Oh, your little adventure." Feliciana raised her eyebrows. "Running off with Miguel. I'll admit it surprised me. A handsome man, to be sure, but so angry and sullen."

"Feliciana! You know very well that Luis and I went by ourselves and found Miguel and Gloria there." She began to cut the dried beef. Miguel handsome? Hmmph. Not in the least. But the memory of the feeling she'd had at Casa Grande rippled through her, his warm hands, his gentle voice. "At least, he's certainly not handsome compared to Nicolas." Because she *had* thought Miguel handsome as he stood on the ruins, gazing out at the desert.

She hacked at the meat. "Nicolas makes me so angry, though. Always telling me what to do, how to act. I shouldn't have been with a strange man, he said. And wearing trousers. How could I?" She chopped the beef harder and faster. "I'll soon be his wife, he said, and he won't tolerate such behavior." Chop-chop-chop. "Huh! Maybe he won't have to tolerate it. Is he my father, to scold me like a child?"

Feliciana laughed. "Watch your fingers."

Mentioning her father slowed Fernanda's chopping. "The worst was Papa's reaction. You should have seen his sorrowful eyes. He said the Marquina family was disgraced in front of Captain Anza and the entire camp. I must set an example for my brothers, he said. That Mama didn't teach me to act this way." She held the knife in mid-chop. "I couldn't look him in the eyes, I felt so ashamed, so childish."

"Don't worry," Feliciana said. "We all do foolish things. At the time, they appear bigger than they are. It will take time for your father to forget, but I'm sure he's already forgiven you." Feliciana patted another tortilla. "As for your marriage to Nicolas, I'll give you one piece of advice. Be true to your heart. You don't *need* marriage. Wait until you're sure."

"Since I was a girl, everyone has been sure that I'd marry Nicolas. But…" She slowly formed the meat into a pile.

"But, *you* aren't sure, Potra?" Feliciana asked gently.

Fernanda dropped pieces of beef, one at a time, into the beans. "I feel as if I'll never be sure," she murmured. "One day it seems the right thing to do. The next day it seems the *only* thing I *can* do." She tossed the entire pile of meat into the pot. "And the day after that, I think if I should marry, it will be like being trapped, locked in a tiny cage, or…or like lacing my chemise so tight I'd suffocate, never to breathe freely again." The words exploded from her lips, and she felt light-headed with relief at having told someone her feelings.

Feliciana continued shaping the tortillas. "I understand how you might feel that way. I promise you, though, marriage doesn't have to mean losing your freedom or yourself."

"I know Nicolas would be a good husband. What other options besides marriage do I have? I suppose I can cook and clean for Papa until we're *both* wrinkled and gray."

Feliciana laughed.

"What of you and José, Feliciana? How did you know it was right to marry him?" Feliciana had told Fernanda that, right before the expedition left Horcasitas, her husband, José, died. Though heartbroken and with two young children, she decided to go on the journey, anyway.

Feliciana laid tortillas on the hot griddle. "I think what you're really asking is how you'll know you're in love. I'll tell you, Potra. Your entire body will know you've found true love. Here…here…and here." She placed a hand on her head, over her heart, and pressed both hands against her stomach. "All the way down to your toes, you will know."

With Nicolas's kiss, Fernanda had felt none of what Feliciana described. The most exciting, the most joyful thing she could think of was riding. Perhaps that's how she'd know if she were in love, her heart would soar like it did when she rode. It hadn't soared with Nicolas. Yet. "So your body told you José was your true love?"

"Yes. My beloved José…we married when I was sixteen. My parents were very ashamed. Their Spanish daughter marrying a low-class mestizo and soldier? How disgraceful. But feelings of love are never shameful. We lived for years under the shadow of that stifling society, those prejudices. That's why we decided to join the expedition, to escape all that. I have hopes that in California my daughters won't have to grow up with such narrow-minded judgment."

"I'm so glad you came, Feliciana, you and your darling daughters. It's true what you say. The people I grew up with in Tubac fought for every drop of Spanish blood so they could call themselves Spaniards. Even Mama wanted us to be known as Spaniards, so she taught us nothing about our Pima ancestry. How brave you were to marry José even though everyone tried to stop you." Fernanda poked the meat into the bubbling beans. "Feliciana, why is it that society approves of Nicolas, nearly a full-blooded Spaniard, marrying me, a mestizo, but didn't approve of your marriage to José?"

Feliciana threw more tortillas onto the griddle. "That, Potra, is something I couldn't answer then, and can't answer now."

After dinner, Fernanda and the other women joined the men and children around the campfire. Marcos was swatting at Luis who, when Papa's head was turned, flicked Marcos's ear, most likely punishing him for revealing their whereabouts the night before. Fernanda ground her teeth to keep from saying some angry comment to her brothers. Is that all they could do while she slaved for them, cooking every meal, cleaning each dish?

As she sat next to Papa, she was surprised to see Gloria and Miguel in the circle. She didn't want to be reminded again of Casa Grande, and was happy the fire camouflaged her face, which she knew must look flushed.

"We convinced Miguel and his sister, Gloria, to join us," Señor Gonzales said. "Another musician is always welcome, eh, Fernanda?"

"Yes," Fernanda murmured. She gave Gloria a small wave and glanced quickly at Miguel, but his head was bowed over his flute as he blew out soft random notes.

Nicolas strode across the camp and sat between Fernanda and her father. "Good evening. It's a fine night, no?" Then he noticed Miguel and his jaw stiffened. He edged closer to Fernanda so their arms touched.

Ramona, sitting at another fire with her family and some others, twisted her head around to look at Nicolas.

Madre de Dios. The girl has no shame, Fernanda thought. *Surely she'll snap her neck if she's not careful.*

Señor Gonzales began to play a spirited melody. Feliciana sang along, and after a few hesitant notes, Miguel joined in with his flute. His shoulders relaxed, his foot tapped out the beat, and his eyes smiled as he played. "A handsome man, to be sure," Feliciana had said. "But so angry and sullen."

Certainly better looking when he's happy, Fernanda thought now.

The song ended, and everyone called for more. Miguel started a slow lyrical tune.

"Fernanda," Señor Gonzales said. "I taught you this song."

"Please play," Gloria said.

Fernanda shook her head. "No, no. I'm not good enough." But she knew she could easily play the song. And she knew the reason she hesitated. It was the way Miguel's lips and fingers made the notes dance from his flute. It was Nicolas sitting so close, his arm tense against hers. It was the three of them together in that intimate circle. She felt Nicolas's eyes on her, and she forced herself to turn to him, away from Miguel's beautiful playing, his softened features…

"Yes, Fernanda, you must play!" The others took up the plea.

Señor Gonzales handed her the guitar, and reluctantly she began to strum along with Miguel's playing. Feliciana joined in, her voice as clear and melodic as the flute. Children danced around the circle of adults who swayed with the music, some closing their eyes as if in a happy dream.

The music filled Fernanda with joy, and the tension flowed from her body. She hunched over the guitar, watching the strings and her hands. With fluid motions of her fingers, she strummed the chords and plucked out the melody. The vibration of the guitar hummed against her thighs and chest; she felt as if she and the instrument had become one, existing only to play music. She looked at Miguel and their eyes locked. In him, she saw the same emotions that flooded her body. The wonder and pleasure of creating music. The thrill of making people laugh or cry with a song. The feel of the instrument in your hands, getting to know it as well as you knew yourself.

Feliciana sang the last note. As if broken from a spell, Fernanda snapped her eyes away from Miguel. She turned to Nicolas amid cries from the group of "Bravo!" "Magnífico!" "Fabuloso!" He was staring at Miguel, his eyes as dark and hot as the fiery coals that separated them. Miguel returned the heated look. Both men appeared ready to leap across the fire and go for each other's throats.

Fernanda stood and brought the guitar to Señor Gonzales. The others were getting up, saying it was time for bed and heading to their tents.

Nicolas walked over to Fernanda. "I'll escort you to your tent."

Although it was just a short distance, Fernanda nodded. At the tent, she opened the flap, but Nicolas stopped her and held her hand. "Sleep well, Fernanda." He hesitated, his mouth opening then closing, as if there was more he wished to say.

Wanting to avoid a serious discussion, Fernanda forced a smile and said pleasantly, "Goodnight, Nicolas." As she crouched to enter her tent, Nicolas tightened his grip on her hand.

"Fernanda..." Emotions—anger, confusion—flitted across his face. Emotions he was obviously trying to hide, to control. But they, and his longing for her, were evident in his eyes.

"Nicolas, I'm tired. Please..." She silently pleaded with him: *I don't want to talk about this now.*

She kicked off her sandals, removed her bodice and skirt, and crawled into her bedroll wearing her blouse, chemise, and petticoat. Papa and her brothers came in, and soon they were asleep. Papa snored as usual, and Ignacio, lying next to her, twitched occasionally from some dream.

Fernanda refolded her rebozo and put it back under her head. She turned on one side and then the other. But she could not sleep. She reached for Miguel's kerchief, which she'd tucked in her bedroll after Casa Grande, meaning to wash it and return it to him. She placed it on her shawl and laid her cheek against it, the cotton soft against her skin. She closed her eyes, breathing in the salty smell of sweat mixed with the smells of the journey: sage and horses and campfires. Turning her face into the kerchief, the odors brought to mind the strength of Miguel's back when he lifted his and Gloria's trunk onto the pack mule, the dark strands of hair that were forever falling loose from his queue, and tonight, his eyes, ignited with passion, gazing into hers as he played his flute.

The next morning, the colonists set off on a trail that took them through Pima pueblos. At each village, the Pimas formed two lines, men on one side of the road, women on the other, and called out greetings. Fernanda's excitement grew when, in mid-afternoon, they halted at a camp on the banks of the Gila River and hundreds of Pimas appeared through the cottonwood trees that lined the river. They crossed the gully carrying firewood, squawking chickens, and blankets. Captain Anza and the interpreter spoke to them, and then the captain announced, "The Pimas have brought gifts of fire-wood, and they want to trade tobacco and beads for chickens and blankets."

Papa and the boys set up the tent, and Fernanda hurried to get water. When she returned to the camp, the Pimas were presenting firewood to Papa. She stopped short and sloshed water from the bucket. Ever since Papa's decision to come on the journey, Fernanda had hoped for this moment. To see Mama's people. To learn of their ways. To talk to them. Now that she finally had the chance, all she could think of was her reserved proper mother dressed like these women.

They wore skirts made of shredded bark, and only their long hair, beads, and paint covered their breasts. How red her face must be, standing with Papa and the other men in the presence of the half-naked women. The Pima men embarrassed her just as much, if not more, with their cotton breeches or blankets caught up between their legs and secured at the waist. They tied a wool cord in their hair and wrapped it back and forth over their heads, forming a crest in which they had stuck feathers, leaves, and flowers.

A group of Pima women linked arms and danced from tent to tent. Across the camp, some Pimas—men and women—were trading with male colonists and soldiers. The scene reminded her of the market in Tubac. What better way to start her communication with the Pimas? Pushing aside her embarrassment, she decided to barter for a chicken for that night's dinner.

As if reading her mind, Luis said, "Papa, do we have something to trade for one of the chickens?"

No! Fernanda wanted to shout. She could make a better deal than Luis. "Papa," she said. "I can barter for a chicken. I have experience from Tubac."

"There aren't any Spanish women trading, only Pima women," Luis said. "The soldiers don't want our women to trade."

She wanted to strangle him so he'd stop talking. Why shouldn't the women trade? Ridiculous! But if she were the only woman…She couldn't humiliate Papa again, not after Casa Grande. Nicolas, too, stood among the soldiers.

Luis started across the camp with some of Papa's tobacco and a chunk of chocolate. Fernanda stopped him, took back some of the tobacco, broke the chocolate in half, and said, "These will get you your chicken."

Luis hesitated, eyeing the items doubtfully. Then he joined the soldiers and Pimas. He soon came back holding a flapping chicken by its legs. He nodded at Fernanda with a grudging respect. "They were pleased with the amount I gave them."

"Good," Fernanda said. But she thought, *In that case, I could have gotten it for even less.*

Nicolas came up to Fernanda and said quietly, "Walk with me. I must go to a meeting soon with the captain, but I'd like to speak with you."

They wandered out of the camp toward the river. When Fernanda saw the river's trickle of water and the soldiers again digging wells, she knew she still wouldn't get her bath. Children played in the almost-dry riverbed, and adults watered their animals in the newly dug wells. Groups of Pimas sat about watching.

Nicolas found a quiet spot, and they sat on the river's sandy bank. He took her hand. "I thought of us when the priest married those couples the other day."

Dread weighed heavily on Fernanda's shoulders. A few days before, Father Font had married three couples who had just met on the expedition. "It was a happy occasion after poor Señora Feliz's death," she said. "But don't you think they rushed into marriage?"

"They're planning now for their lives in California. Why wait?"

"Nicolas, I know what you want to say. But I must finish the journey with my family. I have that responsibility."

Nicolas squeezed her hand. "Our marriage won't interfere with your duties to your family. Your father wouldn't deny us our happiness. I'll speak to him." He moved as if he might go to her father that very minute.

"No, please wait!" For—what? She didn't know, but every time she thought of marriage, she felt like one of the chickens she'd brought home from the market: enclosed in a sack, trapped, suffocating. "Please, I feel we must wait. For Papa…for my brothers."

"You are still…sure about the marriage, Fernanda?" He sounded so unlike himself. Uncertain and insecure.

Now was the time to speak of her doubts. But how could she explain to him when she didn't know exactly what her doubts were. She avoided his eyes and said quietly, "Yes, of course, Nicolas."

Putting his arm around her, he said, "Your father did ask us to wait. I haven't forgotten that. But I'm anxious for our lives together to begin." He lifted her chin. "I do love you, Fernanda." He glanced at her lips. "I've been patient. I can be patient a while longer."

He stood and straightened his jacket with a sharp tug. "Now I must meet Captain Anza." He held out his hand to pull her up. "I'll walk you back to camp."

"I think I'll stay and watch the children play. I see Ignacio and the Rábanos over there."

"Very well, my love. I'll talk with you later this evening."

Fernanda watched him stride away, thinking, as she had so many times before, what a good man he was. She pulled her braid over her shoulder and absently poked her finger through its twists. She knew she was hurting him by not being honest. But how could she be honest when she didn't know what she wanted?

Then she remembered his words, "…duties to your family." She tossed her braid back over her shoulder. Nicolas thought of everything in terms of duty, always the soldier.

Feliciana had said Fernanda must be true to her heart, and that thought made her think of Miguel. The way he looked the night before as he played his flute…But she also remembered his face twisted with hatred when he'd spat the word 'soldier' at Nicolas, when he'd glared at Nicolas across the fire. She sighed. He was such a confusing person. She fingered her rebozo. He was like a complex pattern on a shawl, difficult to see where the weave began or where it ended. Nicolas, though, resembled her simple striped rebozo, the lines of his life going in one direction. The trousers she'd worn represented the difference between the two men. Miguel had approved. Nicolas, of course, had not. But Nicolas, she understood. Miguel, she didn't.

She gazed down the river. The boys still played, forming armies with other children, waving their stick swords in the air. The Pimas watched, laughing and pointing. Then she noticed Miguel. He stood with one foot raised on the riverbank, an arm resting on his thigh, speaking with a Pima girl who sat on the slope. A jolt of jealousy shot through Fernanda, surprising her. She wanted to return to camp and prove to herself that she didn't care. But she also wanted to see Miguel. Whether it was to draw his attention from the girl because of some ridiculous feeling she'd had, or because his presence alone pulled her toward him, she didn't know. But she seemed unable to resist.

As Fernanda approached them, she realized the girl was quite young. Other Pimas lounged under the trees. "Hello," she said.

Miguel straightened, looking surprised and happy. "Hello."

A rush of pleasure filled Fernanda's chest, and she smiled.

Miguel's face reddened. He cleared his throat. "I find I can communicate with my knowledge of the Papago language. It's similar to Pima." He gestured to the girl and a woman and man. "This is Sialik, her mother Ākĕmuli, and her father Ba'ag."

Miguel seemed so comfortable with the Pimas, much more relaxed than he was with the colonists. And how different he was from Nicolas who treated all Indians with such formality. As Fernanda watched Miguel speak with the Pimas, she realized here was an opportunity to question them.

"Miguel, will you ask them about my mother and great-grandmother?"

"I'll try. What do you want to know?"

"I hope to find some Pimas who knew them. Jesuits at the Caborca mission raised Mama after her parents died. She had a birthmark on her cheek in the shape of a blossom. They called her Heosig: Pima for "flower." Her grandmother Suhna didn't live at the mission, but she visited my mother there."

Miguel spoke to Ba'ag. Fernanda held her breath, and then let it escape when the father slowly shook his head. Ākĕmuli spoke and gestured away from the river.

Miguel said, "Sialik's grandfather lived at the Tumacácori mission, near Caborca. They said we might speak to him. Perhaps he'll have some answers."

"Oh, yes, please," Fernanda said.

Ākĕmuli led them into the village, weaving around hens scratching in the dirt and bleating sheep. Men and women, squatting outside grassy huts shaped like halved acorn shells, cleaned hides, repaired tools, or called to children who played among the animals. Fernanda tried to imagine her mother in a village like this, as a small girl before her father died.

Ākĕmuli spoke to an old man who sat cross-legged on the ground outside a hut. He nodded, and Fernanda and Miguel sat across from him. Fernanda peeked inside the hut, but all she saw were dark shapes and shadows.

As Miguel spoke, Fernanda watched the old man's face for any sign of recognition. At one point he nodded, and then he spoke. Fernanda gripped her hands beneath the folds of her skirt, trying to be patient until he finished.

Finally, Miguel addressed Fernanda. "He says he remembers hearing of the girl with a flower on her face, a girl called Heosig. He never met her, though, and he doesn't know of Suhna. He says most Pimas have remained in this area along the Gila River, but some have scattered across the land from here to the Colorado River and beyond. They joined other tribes, marrying into the Yumas, Opas, and others. He says perhaps one of those will know your mother's family."

Fernanda tried to smile at the old man. "Please thank him for me, Miguel."

As they made their way back to camp, Fernanda's feet dragged with the weight of her disappointment. How silly she was to think that, in such a vast land, she'd find someone who knew her mother and great-grandmother. Someone who could tell her what had happened between them so many years ago. "Miguel, thank you for questioning the Pimas. It was kind of you."

"Do you mind if I ask, what are you searching for?"

"I–I told you. I wish to learn more about my mother's people."

"I don't mean to pry, but you appeared to have a deeper reason." Miguel's dark eyes always seemed to say much more than his words, now telling her that she could confide in him.

She'd never told Nicolas about Mama's past, but somehow she felt Miguel would understand. Like her he'd suffered the loss of a parent. Like her he was a mestizo—part of two worlds.

She stopped walking and explained to him what the priests had told Mama about her grandmother abandoning her in the desert. "I feel inside—" she pressed her hands against her stomach "—somehow I feel it can't be true that my great-grandmother would do such a thing. Papa told me they loved each other so." Her voice deepened as she held back a sob. "This is why I must find someone who knows the true story. But it's impossible. Impossible." Tears blurred her eyes, and she hung her head.

Miguel reached for her hands. "Fernanda, look at me. Please." She raised her head. "I'll help you. I don't know how, but I promise I'll help you find the truth. I must warn you, though. I, too, have sought the truth and learned it can bring you happiness, but it can also bring you sorrow."

"What happened, Miguel? Tell me. We can help each other."

"I–I…" He glanced away and his lower lip trembled so slightly Fernanda wasn't sure it actually happened. "No," he said, looking at her again. "What's important now is finding the truth about Heosig and Suhna."

Being so close to Miguel, she could smell his masculine odor from days of not bathing, but the smell was not unpleasant. She became conscious of his hands holding hers, and the feel of his skin against hers made the very center of her body tingle. But she knew the sensations she felt were only the excitement of speaking with the Pima's, of Miguel's offer to help, and her certainty that together they would find the truth.

Chapter Ten

November 3-16, 1775

An unexpected heavy rain fell as the colonists set out the next morning. Fernanda hunched inside her rebozo, but the water soaked through the cotton and trickled down her neck. She shivered. At least with the rains back home, she'd had the dry adobe hut to escape the downpour. Now there was nowhere to go except forward, slowly plodding forward. How she longed to gallop ahead, to leave the others to their sluggish march. Even if she dared, it wasn't possible because, like all the saddle animals, Aletta took slow unsure steps through the slippery soil. She patted the mule. "You haven't had a good meal in days, but don't worry. Captain Anza said there will be plenty of grass at the *lagunas*."

But when they reached the lakes, Fernanda plucked a handful of grass from the salt-caked soil, and then let the blades fall to the ground. "*Galletas*," she said. "Crackers, Aletta. That's your sorry dinner. Grass as salty, stiff, and dry as galletas." She draped her arms around the mule's neck. "Oh, *mi mula*. We're tired, aren't we? Tired of heat and dust and rain. Tired of tasteless food or food not fit to eat. Your poor bones are beginning to show, and probably mine, too, no?" She sighed and petted the animal's coarse hair. "Well, eat and drink what you will before we return to camp."

As the mule sucked up water at the lake's edge, Fernanda noticed the cloudy water and decided not to fill her own bucket. Back at camp, she told Papa about the unclean water.

"The lake water is probably fine for the animals," Papa said. "But I think we should drink from the river."

Fernanda called to Luis and the Rábanos, "Help me carry water from the river to our camp. We can't drink the lake water."

The Rábanos protested. Luis simply ignored her.

"Muchachos, help your sister," Papa commanded. "Now!"

Fernanda marched to the river and, seeing the boys shuffling behind her, snapped, "Hurry, will you? You should help without Papa ordering you."

"You're not my mother," Marcos shouted. "Don't tell me what to do!"

"That's right," Antonio said. "Do you think you're a sergeant commanding his troops?"

"Fine," Fernanda yelled back. "You can look after yourselves. See who will cook your meals and wait on you like a slave."

Luis crossed his arms and made a sound, "*Pffff.* You think we'll suffer without your cooking?"

All the weeks of resentment that had been building inside her exploded, slamming her heart against her chest. "Oh, that's easy for you to say when you sit like a king on his throne waiting to be served. I've tried my best, but none of you care. Always it's the same. *I* do the chores. You do nothing. Well, I'm tired of caring for you. For all of you. Tired, do you hear? Tired!" She stamped her foot, and then stomped on. Yes, *she* had to remain strong; they could whine and complain. It simply wasn't fair. If only she could be free of them, free of them all so she could live her own life as she pleased without their whining and demands, without all the rules about what was correct behavior and what was not, without this rebozo tied around her head. Yes, why must she cover her head? So her skin wouldn't darken? So she *appeared* to be a proper lady? She yanked the shawl off her head and jerked around. Were they coming to help, or would she have to—?

"I want Mama," Jorge wailed. Tears trailed down his face.

Fernanda ran to Jorge and wrapped her arms around his thin body, his shoulder blades like fragile bird wings poking her arms. How could she be so cruel? They were all trying to adjust to life without Mama. She wasn't the only one tired and hungry and wondering when they would ever reach California. She was the oldest, after all, and they relied on her. "I'm sorry," she said, looking at her other brothers over Jorge's shoulder. "I know we all miss Mama." She pulled Antonio and Marcos into her embrace.

"We're sorry, too, Nanda," Antonio said.

Luis gently tugged her braid. "Your cooking's getting much better, Nanda."

Marcos nodded against her shoulder. "The tortillas weren't so dry last night."

Fernanda kissed Marcos's forehead. "Hopefully they'll be even better tonight." Then she held Jorge's hand and said, "Come, who will be the first to reach the river?"

The boys whooped, and, laughing and yelling, Fernanda and her brothers raced across the field and down the bank to the river.

The next morning, Fernanda found Aletta with a bloated stomach. Other animals' bellies had also swelled, and when some of the colonists fell ill, Captain Anza decided the culprit was the salty lake water. He ordered everyone to drink only river water, and all day there was a constant stream of men, women, and children hauling water from the river for themselves and the animals.

Nicolas broke away from his duties to help Fernanda and the boys bring water to their camp. Once, when he and Fernanda were alone at the river, he pulled her into his arms and leaned toward her for a kiss. Fernanda closed her eyes, thinking, *Perhaps this time I'll have the feelings Feliciana spoke of.* But before their lips met, she heard voices, and both she and Nicolas turned to see several people tramping down the bank carrying buckets. One of them was Miguel. He stopped abruptly.

Fernanda pushed out of Nicolas's embrace, and he looked at her with a sharp question in his eyes.

Fernanda ducked her head, feeling her face flush. "Not in front of the others."

Nicolas stared at her for a moment, and then his cheeks became mottled with red and he glared at Miguel.

Miguel, with Gloria behind him, continued toward the river. Gloria paused to speak to Fernanda. "Miguel's horse is sick. We quit watering both our horses at the lake."

"Aletta was sick this morning, but I think she'll be okay," Fernanda said. She glanced at Miguel, who had also stopped. She regretted how she'd reacted when she'd seen him. She'd pushed away from Nicolas almost without thinking. Almost. And now she wanted to sweep the thought from her mind— that she'd done it so Miguel wouldn't see her in Nicolas's arms. "I'm sure your horse will be better soon. He's a strong animal." She spoke to Miguel deliberately using a tone she would with any colonist whose animal was ill.

Miguel's eyes slid from her to Nicolas, the slightest curl of disgust on his lips. "We'll see. Let's get our water, Gloria."

Fernanda felt the sting of Miguel's look as if he had slapped her. It had happened again: The caring man from only two days before had become a hateful, self-righteous…Anger flared in her chest. How dare he judge her? Huh! He thought himself so above the others, so superior to them all.

As Miguel and Gloria walked away, Fernanda glanced at Nicolas. For once it seemed they were of like minds about Miguel, both directing furious looks at his retreating back.

The travelers christened the campsite *Laguna del Hospital*. Three horses died, and the muleteers worked the entire day to drag and bury the horses away from camp. Fernanda busied herself near the tent, not wanting to see the dead horses. Her brothers, though, eagerly watched the event. Madre de Dios! She would never understand boys.

On the fourth day, Captain Anza, worried about the possibility of snow in the mountains, ordered the settlers to pack, and they moved on. The rain stopped and the wind returned. Fernanda used her rebozo to shield herself and Ignacio from the stinging sand that blasted them from all sides. The dust swirled into clouds so thick she couldn't see two horses in front of her. Next to her, riders and horses bent their heads as they plodded forward.

They made little progress, and Captain Anza halted the train. After one night's rest, they set off again. The wind abated, and the captain pushed them into a grueling march of twenty leagues in two days, almost three times what they normally traveled. Fernanda's body had toughened after weeks of riding. And though she'd lost weight, her thigh muscles were stronger and harder. But when they finally stopped to make camp on the bank of the Gila River, and she climbed off Aletta, she cringed at the pain in her stiff legs and her aching bottom.

With grit still crunching between her teeth, and grime covering her like an extra layer of clothing, Fernanda said to Feliciana and Micaela, "Let's see what the river looks like." The other women carried the babies while Fernanda herded Ignacio, Tomása, and Micaela's daughter, Gregoria, down to the river.

When Fernanda saw the flowing water, she said, "We can certainly bathe in this. The women here, and the men…I'll be right back." She ran down the beach, around a bend, and then dashed back to the others. "There's another pool where the men can bathe."

"I'll tell the others," Micaela said, and she climbed back up the riverbank.

Fernanda, taking off only her sandals, sprinted into the water. She dove into a pool, and then burst up gasping for breath. "Freezing!" she yelled. She'd brought Miguel's kerchief and quickly rinsed it, scrubbing out the tiny splotch of dried blood. Back on shore, she peeled off her dripping bodice, blouse, and skirt, draped them over an arrow weed bush along with the kerchief, and then unbraided her hair.

"You're going back in?" Feliciana asked.

"Yes, it's glorious! Cold, but I don't care. At least it will numb my sore muscles." Fernanda splashed back into the river, feeling lighter in just her petticoat and chemise. Ducking below the surface, she scrubbed her scalp. Her dark hair swirled around her face. Her arms glowed with a pale green tint. Just like—just like Mama on that horrible day…

Her flowing hair mingled with blood…Her ghostly skin…Her unseeing eyes…Fernanda launched herself toward shore and crawled out, gasping.

"Fernanda!" Feliciana said. "Are you all right?"

Fernanda nodded. "The river…It's just…I remembered…" She glanced at Ignacio and murmured, "My mother."

"Pobrecita." Feliciana wrapped Fernanda's rebozo around her shoulders.

Fernanda clutched the shawl at her throat. "Thank you."

Ignacio watched her with troubled eyes.

Ignacio relies on my strength, she thought. *He can't see me distressed.* She hugged him, saying, "It's Feliciana's turn, and then you're next!"

Fernanda held Estaquia while Feliciana, hollering, ran into the river. She soon came out, plopped next to Fernanda, and took Estaquia from her. "Does my little one care for a bath?"

The baby wailed, and the women laughed.

Micaela returned, followed by a trail of women and girls. "I'll help Tomása, Gregoria and Ignacio bathe," she said, and she led the children down to the river.

The men's shouts and splashing floated around the bend in the river.

"They sound as if they're enjoying themselves," Fernanda said.

"Oh, ho," Feliciana said, winking. "What a sight that must be."

"Feliciana! Perhaps we shouldn't consider such a sight."

"Come now. You've certainly seen your share of naked men on this journey. For an unmarried woman, you're getting quite a lesson on the male anatomy."

"Yes, I have to admit I'm almost accustomed to the naked Indians." Fernanda poked her toes in the sand. "Feliciana?"

Feliciana lay on the sand with Estaquia sleeping soundly on top of her. "Hmmm?"

"I was wondering…Well, I wondered…I…my mother spoke of marrying my father at fourteen. A frightened girl, she said, but still a woman. Mama was not one to speak of–of physical love. But I knew that's what she meant. I wonder, sometimes, well, about…"

Feliciana opened one eye, smiled at Fernanda, and then closed her eye. "Why is it improper to speak of a natural loving occurrence between a man and a woman?"

"Well, I've certainly been told many times that I'm not a proper lady."

"So, you're wondering if physical love, sexual relations, is frightening, my improper Potra?"

Fernanda's face burned. "I never thought I'd be scared. It's just…I'm wondering, what is it like between a husband and wife?"

"Some women speak of pain the first time, but if there is, it's brief." Feliciana's voice became soft and dreamy. "It's the most beautiful experience in the world. There's the physical pleasure, yes. And what incredible pleasure it is. Better than anything. Better than…chocolate!"

Fernanda laughed. "For me, perhaps, it will be better than riding a horse, because that's the most pleasurable thing I can imagine."

"Yes, that's a good way to define it, better than the best thing you can imagine."

Fernanda scooped up a handful of sand and let it sift over her toes. She loved Feliciana for treating her as an equal, for not laughing at her questions, for being someone she could discuss such matters with.

"But," Feliciana continued, "it's more than just physical pleasure. To be so close to the one you love, to share that love between you, to—for those glorious moments—become as one. That's the real essence of making love." She paused for a moment, and then said softly, "That's how it was for me and my beloved José."

Fernanda touched her friend's arm. "Oh, Feliciana, you must miss him so."

"Yes." She caressed Estaquia. "I do. So much. I thank God I had such a love, if even for a short time." She gently squeezed Fernanda's hand. "I wish that happiness for you, too, Potra."

Will I have such a love with Nicolas? Fernanda wondered. *Or...?*

Gloria scampered down the bank. Ramona followed and, standing near a bush, began to remove her outer clothes and unbraid her hair while talking with some women. Fernanda couldn't help but envy Ramona's beautiful figure, and the reddish highlights in her dark hair that caught the sun and made it shine in spite of days without washing. Unlike Fernanda's black hair, lank and dripping down her chest and back. She was glad the men could not see them.

"Gloria," Fernanda said when the girl approached. "You should bathe. It feels wonderful."

"Perhaps," Gloria murmured. She removed her skirt and blouse, laid them neatly on the ground, and tiptoed into the river. With a yelp, she scurried backward. "Oh, it's cold!" Then she tried again, wincing as she stepped on the small river rocks. She quickly dunked her lower body into the water, squealed, and hobbled over the rocks back to shore.

Fernanda joined her at the water's edge and began to unravel Gloria's long braid. "Let me wash your hair, Gloria. I promise you'll not regret it."

After some protests, Gloria bent her head into the water. Fernanda scrubbed the dirt from her hair, dark and flowing like her own.

Gloria pulled her head out of the water. "The cold makes my head ache, but you're right, it does feel good."

"We'll be clean and beautiful." She raised her voice toward Feliciana. "The men will have someone else to look at besides Feliciana."

Feliciana rolled her eyes, and Gloria giggled. She and Fernanda sat on the shore, and Fernanda began to untangle Gloria's hair.

"I'll try not to pull too hard," Fernanda said. "When we go back, I'll get my comb."

As Fernanda worked on Gloria's hair, a warm blush colored Gloria's cheeks. "It's as if we're sisters," she said.

Fernanda hugged Gloria. Ever since she was little, and brother after brother was born, she had wished for a sister. Perhaps, at least for the journey, she and Gloria *could* be sisters.

Micaela came back with the children, and Ignacio ran to Fernanda, squatted, and played with the top Gloria had given him.

"My brother loves the top," Fernanda said. "I hope it wasn't too precious to part with."

"My father made it for me," Gloria said, watching Ignacio try to spin it on the pebbly ground. "I have others. He made many toys for me, but I had to leave them behind."

"I'm sorry. Your father must have been so talented, and loved you dearly."

Gloria stared at the ground and nodded.

"I can see your brother loves you, too."

Gloria looked up at Fernanda and smiled. "He does. But he treats me like a baby. He wanted me to ask if you would *watch* me here at the river."

Since leaving Laguna del Hospital, she'd barely spoken to Miguel, but then most of the colonists, braced against the terrible weather and strenuous march, had kept to themselves. Still, she was surprised he wanted Gloria with her considering how he looked at her by the river with Nicolas.

"I've noticed he is overprotective, to say the least. If he were my brother, he'd learn soon enough he couldn't control *me*."

She was hoping to make Gloria smile again, but she just shrugged and spun the top for Ignacio.

Poor Gloria. What had happened to her parents? Whatever it was, Miguel obviously felt obligated to protect her to the extreme, although he didn't seem the type to follow rules or rigid discipline. Why had he seemed to approve of her wearing trousers, but then gave that look of disgust when he saw her in Nicolas's arms? Why did he say he was tired of fighting, but seemed filled with a rage he could barely control? Why was he full of such contradictions, and why did she care?

Later, back at camp, Fernanda and Gloria sat next to the fire and finished drying their hair. With her cow-horn comb, Fernanda removed the tangles from Gloria's hair then braided it. Gloria insisted on doing the same for Fernanda. Fernanda sat with her back to Gloria, the fire warming her as Gloria combed her hair. Her eyes were half-closed. She felt drowsy and content.

Gloria said, "Before I braid it, I have a surprise for you. I'll be right back."

Moments later, Fernanda heard footsteps. She lazily opened her eyes, expecting to see Gloria. Instead, Miguel approached. A breeze had picked up, and it pressed his billowing shirt against his broad chest, showing his muscles through the soft cotton. Fernanda realized the better she knew Miguel, the more handsome he appeared to her.

Fernanda tilted her head toward the fire to hide the blush she knew was there. She ran her fingers through her hair to finish drying it. "Gloria just ran off, but she'll return in a minute."

Miguel squatted next to the fire. "Thank you for watching her today."

He seemed to have forgotten her embrace with Nicolas. His face was softened by the fire and a gentle smile.

"She's so sweet," Fernanda said. "I truly enjoy her…" Fernanda stopped combing her hair.

Miguel was staring at her as if entranced by her movements. He had pushed back loose strands of hair from his face, leaving his hand in his hair as he cocked his head to look at her. It was a gesture he did often, and it always warmed her like a cup of sweet cocoa.

"Don't stop," he said. "Your hair…it looks beautiful in the firelight. With it loose, I can see the Pima ancestry in you."

Warmth flushed her face. "I'd be happy to have just a small bit of my mother's beauty," Fernanda murmured. "And I hope to have her wisdom someday, too."

Miguel leaned toward her. "Fernanda, don't you realize you have a beauty and a wisdom all your own?"

His words filled her head. Mama, Papa, Nicolas—everyone it seemed—told her she did things wrong, she should be better, she should act like a proper woman.

Why, just days before, she had vowed once more to try harder. But she failed and failed and failed. She *did* want to be more like Mama and the other women, but was it only guilt and shame that propelled her? Perhaps…perhaps she didn't have to change? Perhaps how she acted, what she wanted from life wasn't wrong. Could what Miguel said be true?

She remembered she'd brought the kerchief, now dry and folded, and handed it to him. "I meant to return it sooner."

As Miguel took the kerchief, his fingers grazed hers. Fernanda's breath shortened with surprise that his brief touch could cause her heart to beat so rapidly. Flustered, she playfully tugged on the kerchief. Miguel grinned and tugged back, and Fernanda tightened her hold. They both laughed, and when Gloria ran up, Fernanda let Miguel take it.

Gloria's hands were hidden behind her back. "I have a present for Fernanda," she told her brother. She danced in front of Fernanda. "Pick a hand, pick a hand!"

Fernanda pointed, and Gloria swung her arm out from behind her back. She held a silky green ribbon embroidered with gold, fancier than any Captain Anza had distributed.

"It's beautiful, Gloria," Fernanda said. "But far too precious. I can't accept it."

"I have others. Please, I do want to give it to you."

"Thank you." Fernanda bent her head while Gloria scooped up her hair and tied it with the ribbon. She peeked through her eyelashes at Miguel. He still watched her, and his face still wore that warm soft look, a look that heated her inside and out more than any fire could.

Chapter Eleven

November 17-21, 1775

The weather was changing, becoming colder with each passing day. Fernanda packed away her sandals and put on her new cotton stockings and leather shoes. Señor Gonzales invited Miguel and Gloria to camp with them. This time Miguel didn't protest, and the others welcomed him and his sister. Fernanda was happy to have Gloria nearby, and she pushed down the faint voice deep inside that whispered the same about Miguel.

She knew Nicolas wouldn't be pleased. Huh! Of course he wouldn't. But it wasn't her doing. *And,* she thought, as if she were already arguing with Nicolas, *with the cold becoming more intense and firewood more scarce, we must combine our resources.* Besides, the gatherings around the communal fire had all but stopped. The families increasingly kept to their own tents for warmth, huddling around small fires, though wood was becoming increasingly scarce.

They passed through more Opa and Pima villages, and Miguel continued to question the Indians about Fernanda's mother. One day, Miguel rode up to Fernanda and offered her a few ears of corn, which he pulled from his saddle bag.

"Fresh corn!" Fernanda said. "Thank you. Where did you get it?"

"From the Pimas in the last village," Miguel said. "And there's a small piece of news about Heosig and Suhna."

"What news? Tell me!"

Miguel held out his hand toward Fernanda, stopping short of touching her. "It *is* small, but hopeful. They told me of old stories they used to hear from Pimas who lived at the same mission as your mother. They said there was one story about an old woman who defied the priests, but they couldn't remember any names or details."

"They could mean my great-grandmother!"

"Yes, they could be talking about Suhna," Miguel said. "They told me the same thing as the old man by the Gila River, that many of the Pimas left the mission and moved to other lands, even beyond the Colorado River. We still have a chance of meeting one of them."

Fernanda stroked Aletta's mane. "I believe we *will* meet one of them. Thank you, Miguel." She dropped the corn into her saddlebag. "Perhaps I'll try making my mother's posole. Hers was the best in Tubac, but I'll admit I'm not known for my cooking."

Miguel leaned on his saddle horn and raised his eyebrows, exaggerating both a casual and prideful air. "I happen to make a great posole."

"Oh, really?" Fernanda laughed. "I find that hard to believe."

"Ask Gloria. It was the best in Horcasitas."

"Well, you'll just have to prove it sometime, won't you?" She eyed Miguel with a tilt of her head, and it seemed as if neither of them could control the smiles that spread across each of their faces.

Nicolas trotted up on his horse, and before he had a chance to speak, Miguel nodded at Fernanda, snapped the reins, and rode off.

"So, what did Indian boy want?"

"Indian boy?" Fernanda fumed. "His mother was from the Papago tribe; his father was Spanish. Yes, a mestizo the same as I in case you've forgotten. Shall you call me 'Indian girl' in that same tone, as if I should be ashamed?"

Nicolas's face flushed red. "I–I'm sorry. I didn't mean anything by that."

"Didn't you? How do you think I feel to have such Spanish superiority thrown at me?"

"I said I'm sorry and I meant it," Nicolas said, sounding irritated. Then his voice softened. "Of course you shouldn't be ashamed. You're beautiful, as was your mother."

As much as it seemed to be a ploy to buy her forgiveness, she knew he was sincere, and she relaxed her tight shoulders.

"Why is he always watching you, though, talking with you?" Nicolas asked, his tone still petulant. "What does he want?"

"He's helping me find out about Mama."

"What does *he* know?"

"He speaks their language."

"And what will happen if you don't find…whatever it is you're looking for?" Nicolas asked.

"Nothing will *happen*. I won't die. The world won't end. But I need to do it for myself. And for Mama." *For that last morning, for the way I acted.* "If I do learn about her Pima life, perhaps I can be close to her as I should have been when she was alive." But her chest ached with the knowledge that even if she did learn about Mama's people, she'd never be able to share it with her mother. "I'm half Pima, Nicolas, and

I know nothing about that part of me. I should have asked my mother, but I didn't."

"You can't keep tormenting yourself about that. Your mother would have told you about the Pimas if she thought it was important."

"But I think it's important."

"Why? Why does it matter? How will it change anything?"

Nicolas didn't seem to understand a word she was saying. Fernanda shook her head. "I don't know. Everything is so mixed up in my mind: Mama's death, this journey, California, what Papa told me about Mama and her grandmother—" She stopped, realizing she still hadn't told Nicolas about Heosig and Suhna.

"You know I'm sorry about your mother, Fernanda. I'd do anything to change what happened."

"I know you would, Nicolas." But it bothered her that he didn't question her about Great-grandmother or any of the other feelings she'd expressed. Whereas Miguel had shown such concern when she told him. Remembering his latest news, a glimmer of hope lightened her heart. Perhaps in the next village they would meet someone who knew Mama's story. Or the one after that...

On the twenty-seventh day since leaving Tubac, the settlers made camp near the Gila River at the foot of a craggy mountain range. Captain Anza was pushing them forward as fast as possible to their next goal: the crossing of the Colorado River, wider, deeper, and faster than the Gila.

That night, Fernanda and her family laid their bedrolls close to a small fire, trying to find sleep and warmth in the increasing cold. In the morning, all the colonists' water containers were frozen, and three cows had died. Their moods improved when they learned that one of the pregnant women, Señora Gutiérrez, had successfully delivered a healthy baby boy during the night. And, of course, the dead cows would provide food. The Rábanos and other children crowded around the muleteers while they skinned and chopped the cows, but Fernanda stayed away, again marveling that anyone would want to watch such a bloody mess.

She soon learned, though, it was the women's job to preserve the meat by cutting it into strips for jerky. Back in Tubac, her family rarely ate fresh beef. When she occasionally brought a chicken home from the market, Mama had been the one to cut off its head, pluck it, and pull out its organs, all in a flurry of squawking, flying feathers, and blood.

Now, as the women worked, queasiness churned in her stomach. Gloria sat away from the women, holding the corner of her rebozo over her mouth and nose. Ramona, too, only made half-hearted cuts in a small piece of meat. Fernanda decided she wouldn't, *couldn't*, act the same. She borrowed Papa's knife and hacked into the bloody raw meat. It was cold, tough, and rubbery. Pieces of hide still clung to some of the slabs and, trying not to gag, she scraped off as much as possible. How could the other women act as if it were not completely dreadful?

Earlier, the soldiers discovered drifts of salt by the river, and the colonists replenished their salt supply. Now, while the women sawed at the beef, children brought them pots of the white powder. They also helped gather wood for fires and strip leaves from smaller branches. Over the smoking fires, the men used the branches to form drying racks for the strips of meat. Following the other women's lead, Fernanda rubbed the strips with salt, and then draped them across the branches.

Surrounded by the fires, she soon became warm. Forgetting her bloodied hands, she wiped her wrist across her sweating upper lip and choked at the sickening smell of the carcass.

Feliciana picked up a corner of her skirt and dabbed Fernanda's nose. "Blood."

Fernanda closed her eyes briefly, said "Thank you," and grabbed another hunk of meat. She forced a shaky smile. "Now, of course, my face will begin to itch. Tell me, why is it always that way?"

The women laughed and, relaxing into the routine of cutting, salting, and hanging the strips, began to chatter.

"We'll stay here at least one more day to finish drying the meat and allow Señora Gutiérrez to rest."

"Oh, isn't he a beautiful baby?"

"Diego Pasqual. A fine strong name."

As the sky darkened, the women finished cutting the last of the meat, and then trailed down to the river to wash the blood and smell from their hands. Crouching at the water's edge, Fernanda looked across the river at spots of fire flickering through the dark silhouettes of the trees. She cocked her head and said, "Shhh!"

The other women stopped talking. The gurgling river, like voices murmuring in the quiet evening, filled the air. Then, the sound of singing drifted across the water.

"The Indians," Micaela whispered. "Their song sounds so sad."

The others muttered their agreement. But Fernanda lifted her face to the stars and white sliver of moon. The song from across the river filled her ears and flowed through her body as if it were part of her blood. Miguel had seen the Pima ancestry in her, and she felt it now, her Pima blood, for the first time. Listening to the faceless voices, she thought it was the most beautiful singing she had ever heard. And she imagined she heard Mama's voice rising above the others, caressing her with its sweetness, enveloping her in a song of love.

Chapter Twelve

November 22-30, 1775

After another day's march, the colonists arrived at the junction of the Gila and Colorado Rivers where several hundred Yumas lived. There they would camp for two days while preparing to cross the Colorado. Captain Anza called everyone to the center of camp to discuss the crossing, and Fernanda stood with Feliciana and her two girls, Gloria, and Miguel. Luis had secured a spot near the captain and Nicolas, and Papa and his brothers stood with him. As the captain began to speak, a group of Yuma men, led by a tall large-boned man, strode into camp. Several of the men, including the leader, wore black blankets draped across their shoulders. Others were naked except for red and black paint smeared on their faces and bodies.

Fernanda watched Gloria dart red-faced but curious looks at the naked Indians. Though Fernanda had told Feliciana she was accustomed to their nakedness, she imagined her face was as red as Gloria's. She looped her arm through Gloria's and whispered, "Men—funny looking, aren't they?"

Gloria blushed again, but giggled.

"Captain Palma!" Captain Anza greeted the tall Yuma man.

Captain Palma embraced Captain Anza, and then each of the priests.

"What a strange name for an Indian," Fernanda said.

"The Spanish officials gave him that name," said Ramona, who stood nearby. She raised her chin and eyed Fernanda down the length of her nose, superior with her knowledge. "He's the leader of the Yumas and has even traveled to Mexico City with Captain Anza and my father."

Mexico City! He's seen more of the world than I, Fernanda thought. Now that they were in Yuma territory, she wondered if they'd meet any more Pimas. And if Captain Palma was an indication of his people, she was sure Miguel would be able to question the friendly Yumas. Perhaps this was one of the tribes a Pima from the mission had joined.

Other Yumas—men, women, and children—came into camp carrying beans, corn, squash, and dozens of watermelons. The women wore bark skirts similar to the Pimas'. Their breasts were naked, except some wore short capes made of pieces of fur woven together with threads of bark. They had pressed their long hair together with mud so it hung stiff and straight. The men also used mud to form the front of their hair into crowns or horns, and they wore the dried heads of giant beetles around their necks.

"I like the women's capes," Feliciana said.

Ramona made a *pffff* sound without looking at Feliciana.

Just to support Feliciana, Fernanda said, "I like them, too."

"Me, too," Gloria said.

Miguel eyed the women with an amused smile.

Ramona put her hands on her hips and said to Feliciana. "And I suppose you would *also* deliberately put mud in your hair?"

"If all the other women did, then I—and you—would, too."

"Never!" Ramona said.

"We all have our customs," Feliciana said. "Don't you think those women are looking at us and saying, 'How can they possibly wear all those clothes!'?"

Fernanda and Gloria giggled. Ramona huffed and then walked away.

Feliciana pointed discreetly at the Yuma men. "And our men would pierce their noses like that."

But that was one thing Fernanda couldn't agree with. "Never!" she said, and Miguel burst out laughing.

Fernanda smiled sheepishly but said to Miguel, "Tell me, can you see my father with the middle cartilage of his nose pierced?"

Miguel laughed again. "No, I guess not."

Fernanda noticed a few men who mingled with the women also wore skirts.

"Why are those men dressed like the women?" Fernanda said, her voice lowered.

Feliciana glanced between the men and Fernanda, as if deciding how to answer. Finally she said, "There are men, such as these, who enjoy dressing as women." She shrugged. "They also might be men who love other men."

Fernanda stared at the skirted males, feeling her cheeks burn. "Oh!" was all she could find to say. She noticed other Spaniards, especially men, eyeing them uneasily.

"You shouldn't be embarrassed," Miguel said. "The Papagos call such men two-spirits: they have the spirit of a man and the spirit of a woman in one body."

Fernanda had promised herself to learn all she could about the Pimas, and now she was curious. "Do you know if the Pimas have two-spirits?"

"I imagine all peoples, not just Indians, have two-spirits," Miguel said.

Feliciana looked at him with respect. "I'm sure you're right."

"In the Papago tribe, they have the honor of giving children lucky names," Miguel said. "They're also experts at weaving and making pottery and baskets."

"You told me the Papagos and Pimas were once a single tribe, so maybe the Pima two-spirits do the same for their people," Fernanda said.

"That could be," Miguel said.

Fernanda looked at the two-spirits from a fresh perspective, no longer embarrassed. They were simply members of their community, and maybe even a little more special than the others.

The Rábanos ran up, and Jorge asked, "Did you see the dead bugs?"

"If only we could wear a pendant like that," said Antonio.

Marcos stared at the beetle heads. "*They* would keep the ghosts away."

Gloria grimaced. "You'd wear one of those?"

"Yes!" the boys said together.

"Hmmm," said Fernanda, eyeing her brothers and then the Yumas. She was forming a plan, but would Papa be angry? Well, he needn't know until she could prove she'd caused no trouble. "Perhaps one of the men would be willing to trade their pendant for something of equal value," she said.

Feliciana tugged her braid. "Potra, what mischief are you up to?"

"I'm going to get my brothers a gift. What's the harm in that?"

The Rábanos, grinning, jabbed each other.

"Wait here," Fernanda said. "I think I know what I can trade."

She ran to her tent, rummaged through the trunk, and pulled out the cow-horn comb Luis had carved for her years ago. The tines were unevenly spaced and different lengths, but she thought the Yumas might find it interesting enough to trade.

She hurried back and held the comb up to Feliciana. "What do you think?"

"See what *they* think."

Fernanda curled the end of her braid around her finger. Perhaps it was a foolish idea. Why would they trade for a silly comb? Perhaps she should forget it. Perhaps she should…

Nicolas and three other soldiers strolled over to the Yumas, and they all used hand signals to communicate. Would she have to deal with Nicolas's disapproval, too?

The Rábanos gave her small shoves, saying, "Go on, Nanda!" "You can do it!" "Remember, one beetle for each of us."

When she still hesitated, Miguel asked, "Why shouldn't you?"

She swallowed her nervousness and, with raised chin and steady gaze, strode over to the men. "Buenas tardes, Nicolas," she said, and nodded to the other soldiers.

"Good afternoon, Señorita," the soldiers said.

Nicolas smiled and stepped close to Fernanda's side. "Did the Yumas bring you food? If not, I'll make sure you get some."

"Yes, vegetables and watermelon. Thank you, though." She picked at the tines of the comb, and then took a silent deep breath and pointed at one of the Yuma's beetle pendants. "Very nice!" She drew her finger around her neck and then tapped her chest. Raising her eyebrows, she held up the comb and gestured between it and the beetle.

The Yuma furrowed his brow, and then nodded and spoke to his companions.

"Fernanda, what do you think you're doing?" Nicolas asked.

"I–I'm bartering with the Yumas. My brothers wish me to trade for some beetle pendants. Is there any harm in that?"

Nicolas scowled. "Captain Anza doesn't want the colonists, especially the women, fraternizing with the Indians."

Another soldier, a sergeant, said to Nicolas, "Leave her alone, Corporal Carrillo. She's right, there's no harm. Besides, I'm curious how she does."

Nicolas gave the sergeant a sharp nod, but his eyes were bright with anger.

The Yuma finally shook his head; he wasn't interested. Fernanda glanced at Nicolas. Should she stop? No, she couldn't give up in the middle of a negotiation. Nicolas was already angry, so why not finish what she'd started?

Hmmm, what else could she trade? She noticed the Yuma men's ornaments in their pierced noses appeared to be status symbols. Captain Palma's nose was adorned with a brilliant blue-green stone. Those close to the leader wore a piece of smooth white bone. These men simply poked a small stick through the hole. *I wonder*, she thought. *Yes, this might please him.* She clutched the comb with one hand and, straining, snapped off one of the tines. She held the tine horizontally just beneath her nose and raised her eyebrows.

The Yuma reached for the tine, and Fernanda let him examine it. He ran his fingers over its surface, which had to be smoother than his twig. Finally, he slipped his pendant from around his neck and gave it to Fernanda. Then he pulled the twig from his nose and stuck in the comb tine.

Looking back at her brothers, Fernanda held up the pendant in triumph. The boys jostled each other, grinning. Miguel was also watching. He caught her eye and nodded with a small smile of approval.

"Well done, Señorita," the sergeant said.

Another soldier nudged her, chuckling. "Now see what you've started."

The other three Yumas were taking off their necklaces. They crowded around Fernanda, holding up the pendants and pointing to the comb. Now she would have one for Ignacio, too!

Miguel came up and said, "Let me help break the tines."

As Fernanda handed him the comb, Nicolas snatched it from her. "I'll do it."

Miguel's eyes blazed and his face flushed, causing his scar to stand out, shiny and pale against the darker skin of his face and neck. Fernanda quickly shook her head at him. He hesitated, and then strode away, his hands closing into fists at his sides.

Nicolas's jaw was tight. Fernanda could see the imperceptible grinding of his teeth. He snapped off three more tines. "That boy is becoming a nuisance." He spoke quietly so only Fernanda could hear. "He'll try my patience once too often."

"Whatever you're talking about, Nicolas, is between you two men." She emphasized the word "men" versus his "boy," and the muscles in his jaw pulsed. As far as she was concerned, they were both acting like boys. "All I wanted to do was trade with the Yumas for my brothers."

He handed her the tines. "I can't deny, you do have an obvious talent when it comes to bargaining." His words should have made her smile, but his disapproval was evident in the tone of his voice—grudging admiration, but also as if he wished it weren't true that she had such a gift, or that she at least kept it to herself.

Later that afternoon, the Spaniards and Yumas gathered in a field overlooking the river for horse races. Later, they would all share a meal of freshly slaughtered cow and the vegetables and watermelons. Fernanda stood with Luis and Gloria, admiring the Yumas' horses.

"Have you ever seen more handsome horses?" Fernanda asked. The animals snorted and pawed the ground: two bays, a black, a dapple gray, and a chestnut, all with muscular limbs and satiny coats. They wore halters and lead ropes, but no saddles.

Captain Anza strode up to the horses. Captain Palma strutted alongside him wearing a shirt, trousers, yellow jacket, blue cape edged with gold braid, and a black velvet cap decorated with jewels.

"It looks like Captain Palma has a new uniform," Luis said.

"He doesn't look very comfortable, does he?" Fernanda asked.

Gloria giggled as they watched Captain Palma occasionally shake his leg in the trousers or tug at the jacket. Fernanda wondered if he wore the clothes just to please Captain Anza.

Two Yumas swung up onto the horses' bare backs.

"Look," Gloria said. "I think they're ready to race."

Fernanda noticed Miguel standing nearby. Would he race? But a soldier and another colonist climbed onto two other horses. Captain Anza, standing with Captain Palma, held a gun in the air and fired. The shot, like a crack of a whip, startled the horses, and they were off.

Yumas and Spaniards shouted, waved their arms, and stomped their feet, urging their favorite on. The horses pounded across the sand. The colonist lagged behind one of the Yumas. The other Yuma and the soldier bounded ahead, neck and neck. They rounded some spiny bushes, kicking up dust so the crowd couldn't see who was ahead. Then they burst through the dust, still even. The crowd yelled louder. Fernanda and Gloria clutched each other's hands. Luis jumped and yelled, his words lost in the frenzy.

The Yuma pulled ahead of the soldier, and with a final spurt, crossed the finish line first. The Spaniards groaned, but shook the Yumas' hands.

"I bet I, or even you, Nanda, would have beat the Yumas," Luis said.

Fernanda playfully pushed her brother. "Oh, even *I*, little brother?"

"Fernanda, look," Gloria said.

Two Yuma girls, close to Fernanda's age, were climbing onto horses.

"Are they going to race?" Fernanda asked.

"It looks that way," Luis said. "But against who?" He nudged his sister. "Fernanda, here's your chance."

"What do you mean?"

"It must be a race for girls." Luis jerked his head toward the Yuma girls. "You can beat them."

"Yes, Fernanda, race," Gloria said.

Fernanda eyed the girls. She might win, and to ride such beautiful animals. What would Papa say? And Nicolas?

Captain Anza called, "They want the women to race, too. Are there any skilled female riders among us?"

"'Nanda, go on," Luis said. "You're our best chance."

Fernanda saw no other women coming forward. Oh, she didn't know. Should she? Shouldn't she? "Do you think Papa would be angry?"

Luis shook his head impatiently. "We're not in Tubac, anymore."

Fernanda took a deep breath, and then called, "I'll race."

Luis and Gloria cheered, and the crowd joined in. As Fernanda approached, she saw Miguel smiling at her, admiration apparent in his eyes.

Captain Anza said, "So, Señorita. Do you know how to handle such a horse?"

Fernanda rubbed her hand over the shiny dark brown coat of a bay horse. It shook its black mane and whinnied. "You're proud, Beauty, no?" To the Captain she said, "Yes, sir. I can handle this horse."

Papa, with Nicolas close behind, pushed his way through the crowd. A deep line furrowed between her father's brows. "Fernanda," he said quietly, "will you insult your mother's memory? You know she didn't approve of this type of riding."

"I do know, Papa, and I don't want to hurt you, either. But you encouraged my riding when I was a child. You told me I had a special way with horses. Why did that change simply because I'm older?"

Papa's lips remained tight, but he glanced at her and then the horse.

She clasped his hand. "Don't you see, Papa? A new life awaits us in California. All our skills, men and women, will be needed." Her voice softened. "Things won't be the same as they were in Tubac. I think Mama would have realized that."

Papa's stiff shoulders relaxed. "My little girl has grown into a wise woman. And a persuasive one." He grasped her shoulders, his eyes showing resignation, and then respect. "Good luck, Mi'ja."

Fernanda bounced up and kissed Papa's cheek. She glanced at Nicolas.

He nodded, and then said, "Good luck," though he didn't look pleased.

She turned to Captain Anza. "I'm ready." She reached up to the two Yuma girls, smiling, and they shook her hand. One of them grinned, her eyes friendly but also showing a competitive gleam. A soldier offered his bent knee to help Fernanda onto the horse. No one else had volunteered to race, so the three girls lined up their horses. Captain Anza raised his pistol, shot into the air, and the horses burst forward.

The crowd erupted into cheers. Fernanda squeezed her calves into the horse's side. "Ride, Beauty, ride!" She leaned closer to the horse, urging it forward with her words and body. She darted glances at the other riders. Both pounded a horse's head-length ahead of her. *Oh, no! Don't watch them. Concentrate on riding.*

She galloped toward the bushes where she'd make the turn. The other two horses rounded the mark, kicking up a cloud of dirt. Fernanda, close behind, blinked the dust from her eyes. She pulled back on the lead rope and sat upright to slow the horse for the turn. Not slow enough! The horse's shoulder dropped, and Fernanda slid on its back, losing control. They were going down. No! She kept her inside leg glued to the horse's side and pulled the lead rope, her arm muscles straining against the downward slide of the horse. "You can do it, Beauty, you can do it!" The horse flicked its ears as it regained its footing. Fernanda squared her shoulders, and as they came out of the turn, she hunched forward, dug her heels in the horse's side, and charged down the straightaway.

The other horses were almost a full length ahead. Shouts, like irregular beats on a drum, pounded against her eardrums: "Go—Nan—Fast—Win—No—Lose!"

She gritted her teeth and closed her ears to the voices. Murmuring over and over, "Go, Beauty, we'll catch them, Beauty, go, Beauty," she stretched forward and squinted, the crowd becoming a blur as she raced toward the finish. The memory of riding came back to her: Her love of galloping across the plains in Tubac, her feeling of oneness with the animal. She squeezed her legs tighter against the horse's sides. The horse responded and charged ahead. Its driving legs pounded against the earth. Fernanda dared to glance to her left. She was gaining on one of the Yuma girls. Darting her eyes to the right, she saw the second girl was falling behind. The race was now between her and the other girl!

She leaned lower, her braid streaming down her back, her skirt plastered to her legs. *Go, go. Almost there!* She was nearly even with the Yuma. The other horse's ears lay flat against its head. The sound of eight hooves pummeled Fernanda's eardrums, deafening her to any other noise.

Then, the finish line. She had crossed it! The crowd was cheering. She swung her head, left then right. *Who won? Who won?* Luis, grinning, pulled her from the horse. Gloria grabbed her arm, jumping up and down.

"Did I win? Did I win?" Fernanda asked.

Luis shouted above the crowd. "No, second. But what a race, what a ride. Nanda, you were fantastic!"

Fernanda held her hand over her trembling mouth. Her entire body vibrated. She laughed loudly. Oh, she wanted to scream with joy. It *had* been a fantastic ride. The Yuma girl who had won waved to her. Fernanda waved joyously back, and then headed toward Papa and Nicolas, pushing through the crowd amid cries of "Bravo, Fernanda!" and pats on the back.

A voice close to her ear said, "You were born to ride. I can see it's in your blood." She was forced forward but she glanced over her shoulder. It was Miguel who had spoken. The cries of the crowd became an indistinct roar in her head. Dizzy, she swayed for a moment. That look on his face, as if he knew her better than anyone else.

Then she stood before Papa. He squeezed her arm. "Fine riding, Mi'ja. You made the family proud in front of the captain—" A roar from the spectators interrupted him. "Another race," he said. "It looks as if Vicente Feliz will compete. Let's see if he does as well as you."

He disappeared into the crowd, and Nicolas stepped forward. Clasping her hands, he said, "I've never seen a woman ride with as much passion as you, Fernanda. I have to say, it was an impressive thing to watch."

"Thank you, Nicolas. Oh, it was glorious to ride again!"

He chuckled and pushed a loose strand of hair from her forehead. "I was reminded of you as a young girl, always so impulsive, going headlong into any challenge."

Fernanda warmed to the admiring and proud look in Nicolas's eyes.

"Look at you now," he continued. "Grown into a beautiful woman." Then he winked. "Of course, you'll have to leave this impulsive behaviour behind once we're married, so get it out of your system now. You'll have more important things to do when you have a home and children to care for."

The smile on her face, the warmth she felt from Nicolas's adoring look, and the thrill of the ride all faded with the shock of his words, freezing the happiness inside her as suddenly as if she had jumped into the frigid river.

Chapter Thirteen

December 1-3, 1775

Fernanda rummaged through the trunk for her new clothes. Earlier that day, they had crossed the Colorado River, a slow and tedious process with so many people to get to the other side of the wide river, a distance of over one hundred horses nose to tail Nicolas had told her. But they'd accomplished it with no mishaps, and Feliciana had convinced everyone they must have a fandango to celebrate. Everyone except Father Font, who voiced his objections. But Captain Anza had given his approval.

Papa and the boys had gone ahead to the party, leaving Fernanda alone to dress. As she pulled out her clothes, she remembered when Feliciana had told her, on the day they first met, that they might have a fandango. Fernanda laughed quietly; she had not believed Feliciana. Now, she slipped into her white petticoat, loving the feel of the cotton. It was stiffer, rougher than her old one, but so clean, so new. She stepped into her skirt and pulled it up while shaking her hips so the petticoat fell beneath the skirt. And the blouse, what beautiful embroidery it had. Once dressed, she pulled the broken cow-horn comb through her hair, humming, imagining the men's surprise when they saw the women in all their new finery.

Fernanda did feel pretty, and alluring. She swayed her hips, picturing Nicolas trying to sneak another kiss. They hadn't spoken again about the race, but he'd been so helpful to the family and attentive to her, she had pushed his comment to the back of her mind.

She rustled through the trunk, grabbed two ribbons—the red one and the green one Gloria had given her—and wove them through her braid. The braid draped over her shoulder, and the ribbons streamed past the end of her hair. She picked up the ribbon ends and let them flow through her fingers, suddenly imagining Miguel's face when he saw her. Would his eyes widen in surprise at her hair, her new clothes? And then it was Miguel she saw in her mind, not Nicolas, who whispered she was beautiful, whose lips parted, pulling her toward him for a kiss…

She dug deeper into the trunk and pulled out the new rebozo, bringing with it another, older one. "Mama's," she whispered. She draped it over her shoulders. Papa would be pleased if she wore it to the dance. But she eyed the new shawl with its royal blue and green embroidery and golden fringe. "All of us will look beautiful tonight," Feliciana had told the women. After days of traveling, dirt, and dust, Fernanda longed to look beautiful. Mama would understand. Still, she hid her guilt along with her mother's rebozo at the bottom of the trunk.

Outside the tent, no one was in sight. She twirled, and the pleated skirt billowed around her. She felt she could fly away into the night, like a poppy plucked from the desert floor and caught up in a hot Sonoran wind. The sound of music and singing flitted over the tops of the tents. She started to skip toward the fandango when some other noise stopped her—singing, drums, and other instruments—coming from the Yuma village across the sandy field and beyond a row of willow trees. Fernanda hesitated, listening to the laughter and shouts of the Spaniards' dance. Then she turned in the direction of the Yumas.

She walked across the field, the moon lighting the way around scrubby creosote and ash-colored burro weed. When she reached the grove of trees, she saw light from several fires flickering through the branches. Fingering one of the narrow willow leaves, she wondered if she should go on. What would they think when they saw her? Would she appear rude for interrupting their celebration? How would she speak to them? And why hadn't she thought of these things before coming?

A new song wafted through the rustling leaves, reminding her of the Pimas' song that had filled her with such a feeling of beauty, of affinity with the Indians. Forgetting her hesitation, wanting to be a part of their celebration, she parted the branches and stepped into an opening, into the Yuma village.

Three fires burned in the center of the clearing. Their flames reached for the black sky, flinging sparks up to the blazing white-hot stars. Hundreds of Yumas sat on the ground in a large circle outside the fires. Some faces shone bright in the firelight. Others wore eerie masks created by firelight and shadows. And many were only visible by a dark silhouette. Sitting closest to the fires were the musicians. A few men played a slow wistful song on their flutes. Other men beat a muted rhythm on overturned baskets. Women softly shook gourd rattles, while others scraped roughened or notched sticks against one another to create a sound like the buzz of cicadas on a hot afternoon.

The Yumas swayed and began to sing. Fernanda stayed in the shadows of the trees, but she too rocked to the music.

Closing her eyes, a vision of Mama cradling Ignacio in her arms floated in Fernanda's mind. Yes, a lullaby. It must be a lullaby.

Abruptly, the music stopped. The drummers picked up sticks and struck the drums with a rapid beat. Many of the Yumas, surely one hundred or more, hopped up and formed a circle around the fires, draping their arms across each other's shoulders. While the other musicians picked up the driving beat of the drummers, the dancers raised their feet and stomped in unison around the fires. The thick bark strips of the women's and two-spirits' skirts rustled and rattled like another musical instrument. The dancers raised their faces to the sky and sang. Fernanda didn't understand the words, but she understood the joy on their faces. Entranced by the vibrant music and dancing, she tiptoed closer to the celebration.

The circle of Yumas danced past her, each face illuminated by a nearby fire. The men had decorated their faces and bodies with blue and black paint, the women with red. A girl, her face painted red with two rows of white round spots on each cheek, broke from the circle and rushed to Fernanda. Her eyes sparkled, and she spoke excitedly to Fernanda. Then Fernanda realized she was the girl from the race, and they clasped hands, both grinning. The girl tugged Fernanda toward the circle. Fernanda pulled back, embarrassed to dance with the Indians. She should get to the fandango; Papa, everyone would be wondering where she was. But…She *was* at a fandango. Why shouldn't she dance here, then return to camp? Here, for her Pima half, for Mama. At the camp, she'd dance for her Spanish half.

She let the girl pull her into the circle, and she followed the simple dance steps. The other dancers looked at her curiously, but they continued with their song. Fernanda realized they repeated a chorus, and after a few rounds, she joined in.

The girl squeezed her hand, and each time the chorus came, she and Fernanda sang together with the happiness of newfound friends. When the dance ended, Fernanda backed away from the circle. The Yuma girl walked with her. Fernanda gestured toward the faint sound of the Spanish music then waved, saying goodbye.

The girl pointed at herself and said, "Aqwaq."

That must be her name, Fernanda thought. She placed her hand on her chest and said, "Fernanda."

Aqwaq bent her head, removed a necklace, and handed it to Fernanda. A chevron shell with a hole punched in it hung from a string of rawhide. Surely it must be precious to the girl. The traders from the Baja California coast didn't find their way to that part of New Spain very often.

"I can't take this, Aqwaq," Fernanda said, shaking her head.

Aqwaq said something, took the necklace, and slipped it over Fernanda's head.

Fernanda picked up the chevron and whispered, "Thank you." Rubbing her finger over the ridges of the shell, she thought, *I should give her a gift in return. But I've nothing to give; nothing except...my new rebozo. I have two others, my old one and Mama's.*

The faint sound of a guitar and laughter touched her ears. She pictured the fandango, the women twirling in their new clothes, beautiful and colorful as scattered flower petals. She loved the new rebozo and wanted so much to look beautiful, too.

"I should go." Fernanda hugged Aqwaq. But her selfishness made her feel small against the grandeur of the star-dusted night, the beauty of the music and brightness of the dancing, the joy of connecting with Aqwaq and the other Yumas. She touched the necklace as she walked back to the trees. She would make it up to Aqwaq and bring her something special tomorrow. She turned and waved one last time, and then parted the branches and left the Yuma village behind.

At the camp, small groups of people warming themselves by small fires formed a larger circle around an area left open for dancing. There, in the center, stood Feliciana with her arms raised behind her head, swinging her hips and singing a saucy ballad accompanied by guitars, small drums, and flutes. Father Font watched, scowling. Obviously, he didn't approve of Feliciana's performance, although everyone else, including the other two priests, was laughing and clapping.

Fernanda settled between Papa and Ignacio. Her other brothers also sat cross-legged around the fire, along with the Feliz family, the Gonzales's, Gutierrez's, Gloria, and Miguel.

"Nanda, where you been?" Ignacio asked.

Fernanda hugged him, avoiding the question and Papa's raised eyebrows.

When she didn't answer, Papa handed her a plate of food. She felt too excited to eat, but the unexpected sight and smell of sausage made her mouth water, and she took a bite.

"Captain Anza ordered extra rations tonight for our fiesta," Antonio said, stabbing a piece of sausage with his fork.

"And wine," Señor Gonzales said. He handed Fernanda a cup.

She eyed Papa, and the señor laughed. "A little will not harm her."

Papa shrugged, and Fernanda took a sip. The wine burned her throat, but settled warmly in her stomach. Señor Gonzales strummed his guitar, and Miguel began to play his flute. Fernanda again sipped the wine, stealing a glance at Miguel. He raised his eyes to her as he played, and she quickly looked away. She hadn't spoken to him or Nicolas since the race yesterday. Her stomach fluttered each time she remembered Miguel's words: *You were born to ride.* And her stomach knotted each time she remembered Nicolas's: *Get it out of your system now.* She scanned the groups for Nicolas and saw him standing around a fire with other soldiers.

"Where *have* you been?" Gloria said. "I thought you would miss the dancing."

Papa eyed her. "The time you took has paid off. You look beautiful, Mi'ja."

Fernanda leaned close to his ear and whispered, "Papa, I'll tell you about it later. I visited the Yuma village."

A series of expressions crossed her father's face: surprise, curiosity, something close to anger, and then with a shake of his head, resignation.

Fernanda bit her lip. She was truly a troublesome daughter. Poor Papa.

Señor Gonzales handed his guitar to Fernanda. "Here, Fernanda. You play. My fingers need a rest."

Fernanda strummed a few songs while the last of the colonists joined the party. The musicians picked up the pace of their music. Fernanda, unable to keep up with them, gave the guitar back to Señor Gonzales. Feliciana again went to the center of the circle, and her feet moved in intricate steps to the hard, fast strums of the guitar. A man joined her, stepping and clapping with his hands in the air as he circled around her. More people jumped in, and soon the area was swirling with dancers.

Fernanda leaped up and grabbed her father's hand. "Come, Papa. You must dance, too."

Papa chuckled and shook his head. "Me? No, no. I'm too old for such things."

Fernanda purposefully puffed out her lower lip. "If you don't dance, neither will I, and you'll spoil all my fun."

Papa slapped his palm across his chest. "Ah, Mi'ja. You know how to wrench your poor father's heart. We shall dance."

Fernanda kissed his cheek then pulled him into the middle of the clapping stomping dancers. Feliciana twirled past. Then Gloria. Micaela looped her arm through Papa's, swung him around, and moved on. Papa caught the excitement and wove through the crowd, performing a fancy jig that made Fernanda gasp with laughter. She had never seen her father so unfettered.

She skipped and danced, looping arms with Feliciana, Señor Feliz, and Luis. Then Miguel hooked her arm, and they swung around and around, Fernanda laughing and squealing. He grabbed her hands, and they kicked through the crowd. He twirled her, then put his hand at her waist and guided her around the other dancers. She dropped her head back, staring up at the swirling stars, her heart bursting free. What a glorious evening! She spun past Nicolas who stood at the edge of the dancers. Ramona stood next to him, talking and wiggling her hips, probably trying to entice him to dance. But he only had eyes for Fernanda. Fernanda smiled at him and thought, *Oh, I should stop and pull him in to the dance.* But she was having too much fun. And Miguel…his eyes…his touch…

A hand clutched her arm. Her smile faltered as she turned to see Nicolas staring at Miguel, his eyes full of hatred. He said to her, "It isn't proper for you to dance with other men when we're betrothed."

Fernanda's chest heaved from the exertion of dancing. Her head still spun, and she pressed her palm against her forehead.

Miguel placed his hand at the small of her back as if to steady her, and Nicolas's hold on her arm tightened.

She yanked her arm free, and stepped away from both men. "There's no shame in dancing, Nicolas. You can't keep telling me what I can and can't do! And I'd prefer to discuss our affairs in private. Besides, we're not officially betrothed."

Nicolas's face paled, turning white like the moon against a dark sky. "Fine," he said between clenched teeth. "Let's discuss it. Now. Away from here."

"That's ridiculous. Huh! We're in the middle of a fandango." She had forced the laugh, but tears of anger and desperation choked her words. She glanced at Miguel and saw the hatred for Nicolas radiating from his face, his entire body. Oh, why had she let this happen?

"I see. Now I'm ridiculous." Behind Nicolas's glare, his hurt was obvious. "Sometimes I don't know who you are, Fernanda."

"Perhaps that's your problem," Miguel said.

Nicolas clenched his fists. "What did you say?"

"I said, that is your problem. You *don't* know who she is. You treat her as if you own her—soldier." Miguel spat the word in his usual way.

"You can't speak to me that way, you worthless—"

"Worthless? You and all your kind are worthless." Miguel's mouth twisted, as if he might snarl.

Nicolas's face all but exploded in a fury of red. "I've had enough of your insolent ways, you spineless coward."

"We'll see who's the coward."

And before Fernanda could stop them, the two men were in the dirt, rolling and punching, grunting and cursing. The music and dancing stopped.

Fernanda screamed. "Stop, please stop!"

Nicolas slammed his fist into Miguel's eye. Miguel punched Nicolas in the stomach and then in the mouth. Papa and another man ran over and tried to break up the fight. Two soldiers jumped in, one grabbing Miguel, the other Nicolas, and pulled them away from each other. One of Miguel's eyes was beginning to swell, and Nicolas's lip and nose were bleeding. A soldier gave Miguel a hard shove. Miguel stumbled, but managed to stay on his feet. Both soldiers walked Nicolas back to the barracks.

Papa called, "Play, play! Everything's fine. Continue with the fandango." And then to Fernanda, he said, "Mi'ja, come sit with me by the fire."

Miguel tried to take Fernanda's hand, but she clasped her hands behind her back. "I'm sorry," he said. His swollen eye was now just a slit. "I didn't mean for that to happen. It's just him…how he treats you."

Fernanda, hurt and saddened because the beautiful night was ruined, and disgusted with both men, could barely bring herself to look at Miguel. "I thought you were sick of all fighting," she said, and then, turning her back to him, said to her father, "Papa, I'm tired. I think I'll return to the tent."

Papa took her elbow and escorted her away. Over his shoulder he said to Miguel, "See to that eye before it's completely swollen shut."

Alone in her tent, Fernanda sank onto her mat and dropped her head into her hands. Her head ached, probably from the wine, but her heart still pounded in her chest from anger and humiliation. Madre de Dios! She'd had enough of both men. Men? They were children, little boys. She ran her fingers through her hair, and then yanked on the ribbons, trying to rip them from her hair. But she only made her headache worse.

She took a deep breath and began to unravel her braid. It made her feel ill to see either one of them hurt. But each time she thought of their foolish, ridiculous behavior, she became furious all over again.

Before the fight, though…dancing with Miguel had been like floating on happiness. She hadn't wanted it to end. And he'd defended her against Nicolas's controlling ways. Why couldn't Nicolas have let them be? She *would* have danced with him during the next song.

Fernanda stretched out on the mat and stared at the roof of the tent. She knew Nicolas truly loved her, but he shouldn't have fought with Miguel. And then the words she'd thrown at Nicolas about their marriage hit her with a cold wave of guilt. She may as well have slapped his face in front of Miguel and the entire expedition. He infuriated her, but he didn't deserve that. He owed her an apology, but she owed him one as well. Tomorrow, she'd tell him she was sorry, and she hoped he'd say the same to her.

As she drifted off to sleep, she wondered how Miguel was doing, if Gloria was taking care of his eye, if he'd be able to see out of it in the morning, and if he was thinking of her at all…

The next morning, tired and groggy from the celebration and wine the night before, Fernanda came out of the tent rubbing her eyes, her mind swirling with thoughts of Aqwaq and the Yuma dance, and worst of all, the fight between Miguel and Nicolas. But she had no time to think. Captain Anza had an important announcement to make, and she hurried to join the assembled colonists.

Standing on a boulder, the captain announced, "On the march ahead, we'll find scant water and pasturage. In order to conserve these resources, I am splitting the expedition into three divisions."

The colonists murmured in surprise, and as the captain explained further, the tension in the group of travelers was palpable. Each division would leave one day apart so the springs could replenish the watering holes before the next division arrived. The pack and saddle animals would be divided among the three divisions.

Fernanda's family was assigned to the first division along with the other colonists, including Gloria and Miguel, he with his swollen, purple eye. Soldiers with families would also leave first, and the captain and Father Font would lead that division. Twelve soldiers, commanded by Sergeant Grijalba, would march in the second division. Lieutenant Moraga would lead the third division of twelve more soldiers. Father Garcés and Father Eixarch would stay with the Yumas to teach them Christianity.

Nicolas stood in the group of soldiers awaiting their assignments. All color and emotion had been washed from his face; his lip was puffy and bruised. He wouldn't look in Fernanda's direction.

As Sergeant Grijalba and Lieutenant Moraga chose their men, Luis said, "The third division will have the most difficult time. Water and pasturage could be used up by the time they arrive at the campsites."

Nicolas, one of the last to be called, was assigned to the third division.

Chapter Fourteen

December 4-19, 1775

The icy wind ripped Fernanda's rebozo from her frozen fingers. She snatched it back, clutched it under her chin, and hunched over Ignacio, trying to protect him from the wind's ferocious attack. With two wool petticoats layered over the cotton one, wool gloves, and a wool cloak, she was still cold.

Squeezing her calves into Aletta's sides, urging the mule forward, she stared across the plain at the mountains that loomed ahead. Clouds slumped like bundles of wet dark wool over the snowy peaks. If it was cold now, what would it be like in the mountains?

More than a week had passed since the fandango. Fernanda had completely forgotten to bring a gift to Aqwaq. Nicolas, Miguel, and what had happened at the dance dominated her thoughts.

She winced as another blast of wind stung her cheeks. During the past week, at least ten horses had died from the freezing temperatures. A few emaciated Indians, so different from the Pimas and Yumas with their smiles and warmth, came down from the mountain and stole two more. Soldiers recovered them, but Fernanda didn't blame the Indians. She imagined trying to survive in this cold barren land. Miguel continued to question the Indians they encountered, and Fernanda kept a spark of hope alive.

Luis rode up to her, his nose red and lips white, his face raw and chapped from the cold. "Captain Anza is halting the train up ahead. He says there's no use going on in this wind."

Fernanda nodded, and Luis continued spreading the word to the other travelers. Since they had split into three divisions, he found every opportunity to help the captain and soldiers, probably hoping to prove himself to the soldiers he admired.

The colonists stopped near a marshy area with grass and underground springs. After soldiers dug wells for the animals, Fernanda crossed the spongy ground to take Aletta for a drink. Cold water seeped through her leather shoes, and she climbed onto the mule. While the mule sucked up water, Fernanda breathed onto her hands and wondered how Nicolas was faring. Was he staying warm? He'd been trained for hardship, so he should be fine. But her shoulders sagged, heavy with worry for his welfare, and guilt for what she'd said to him at the fandango.

The wind calmed some, and the travelers quickly set up camp, deciding to share tents because of scarce firewood. Feliciana and her girls joined Fernanda's family, Gloria and Miguel stayed with the Gonzales's, and the Gutiérrez's shared the Feliz tent.

Before daylight ended, gray clouds rolled across the sky like tumbleweeds, crashing and clinging together until they covered the sky in one dark mass. Fernanda imagined the clouds as giant canvas bags, filled and ready to burst with their burden of stinging snow. What would it be like to be surrounded by something so cold, so frozen? How did the Indians, with their scant clothing, survive? *Well, they do,*

Fernanda thought. *So we will, too, with our petticoats, trousers, and leather shoes.*

As soon as Papa pounded the last stake into the ground, the wind began to blow. They scurried into the tent. Luis built a small fire, adding another piece of the precious wood only when the last log crumbled into a few red and black coals.

The young children drifted off to sleep. Papa, Feliciana, Luis, and Fernanda, too cold to sleep and wanting to keep the small fire burning for some warmth, stayed awake. The wind whistled through every small opening of the tent. Well into the night, their wood ran low and Luis ventured outside to find more.

He popped back inside, a flurry of snowflakes chasing him into the tent. "It's snowing!"

Fernanda dashed to the tent opening. Nothing was visible except the slanting curtain of slushy snowflakes that stung her face. She flung the flap closed and hurried back to the fire, wiping the melting snow from her face, her cheeks as cold as the icy drops.

"We may not travel tomorrow if this weather continues," Papa said.

"I hope not," Fernanda said. "The children can't ride in this wind and snow." She glanced at the others, their faces sagging with fatigue, thin and old-looking—even Luis—from the poor food and bad weather. She must look the same. Her skirt hung looser around her waist with each passing day. She forced a smile and said, "At least we don't have to worry about a water shortage."

Papa chuckled softly. "That's true, Mi'ja, that's true. Now let's try to get some sleep."

Fernanda snuggled under the blanket with Ignacio. Listening to the moaning wind, she stared into the last glowing coals of the fire. If they stayed there tomorrow, perhaps the three divisions would be reunited. She never liked the idea of separating the expedition. And Nicolas…The way they parted saddened her and caused a gnawing in her stomach that never quite went away.

A blast of wind shook the tent flap and a small drift of snow snuck inside. Fernanda held Ignacio closer. She couldn't lessen her fear of the cold mountain passes that awaited them. She closed her eyes and pictured her home and garden in Tubac, her mother in the heat of the summer kitchen preparing dinner. The memory squeezed her heart. No, no. She wouldn't think of that. She forced her mind to create other images— green hills, rich earth, sunshine—all she'd been told to expect in California. Eventually, she fell asleep.

Fernanda awoke, shivering. Frosty light seeped through the canvas walls. Yawning, she slipped away from Ignacio, deciding to find some wood before the others wakened. She put on her shoes, cloak, and gloves, draped her rebozo over her head, and tiptoed out of the tent, stopping short at the sight of the snow.

Although the sky was overcast with a steel gray, she squinted against the glaring whiteness that covered the ground, rocks, and shrubs: as bright as an expanse of sand in the sunlight, but oh, so cold! And so quiet. Once, wishing for privacy away from her family, she had snuck to the back room of their hut and covered her ears to seal out all noise. Still she heard something: her breathing, her heartbeat, her thoughts. But here, now, there was not a single sound.

She stepped across the frozen ground, the crunch of her footsteps breaking the cottony silence. At the well, each blade of grass was covered in its own icy sheath. The watering holes were coated in a thin layer of transparent ice. She threw a stone and it cracked the ice into an intricate web then disappeared into the dark jagged hole. A twig snapped behind her. She took in a sharp cold breath when she saw Miguel approaching. He, too, wore a wool cloak and gloves.

"You're up early," he said.

"I couldn't sleep." Fernanda pulled her rebozo tightly around her head and shoulders. "It's so cold, but the snow is beautiful. I had no idea it would look like this."

"Yes, it is beautiful. I thought this morning, how can something so wondrous be so harsh?" Miguel picked up a rock, aimed it at the hole Fernanda had created, and shot it straight through. They grinned at each other like two children sharing in their own secret game. There was an awkward silence. Fernanda picked a blade of frozen grass.

Miguel said, "Since water isn't a problem any longer, the captain's decided to wait for the other divisions."

"Oh! I think that will be much better for us to travel again as a group."

"You're concerned about Nicolas." It wasn't a question.

"For him and all the soldiers."

"He said you and he were betrothed."

Fernanda heard the tension behind his deliberate even tone. She picked up a twig, shook off the snow, and broke it in half. "And I said no final decision had been made."

"It *is* your decision to make, correct?"

She snapped her head toward him in anger. But she thought, *How does he always seem to know my deepest concerns?*

When she gave no reply, he said, "Fernanda, I didn't mean…it's just that…" He rubbed his face and quietly groaned.

Something about his manner, his tone, made Fernanda's heart quicken. Even in the midst of the biting cold, heat inflamed her chest and spread up to her face.

"It's just that, I wondered if you were truly betrothed because…" Miguel took her hand. Fernanda hesitated, and then looked up at him. His sculpted face seemed to have softened, his eyes the color of dark cocoa and just as warm. He bent his head closer to her face. "Fernanda, I—"

His breath was hot against her lips. He kissed her, and in spite of the cold, his lips were heated, a soft flame against her own, and she wanted the kiss to go on forever. He put his arms around her, pulling her close, deepening the kiss, and she relaxed, melting, her body tingling like it did when she bathed in the river, only she was warm not cold.

Excited shouts echoed from the camp. Fernanda pushed away from Miguel, but let her hands linger on his chest. His eyes widened with surprise and then desire. He grasped her hand and tried to pull her back. She shook her head and turned toward the shouts. "The others have discovered the snow," she said.

"Fernanda, there are things we need to discuss."

Not now. Not now. "I must go help with breakfast. They'll be looking for me."

"Promise me we'll talk. Soon."

"Miguel, I can't think straight. I–I…yes, yes, I promise." Then she asked gently, "Are you coming?"

"No, I'll gather firewood for tonight." As she walked away, Miguel said, "Fernanda, I can't apologize because I'm not sorry. But, I must know. Are you angry?"

Fernanda stopped and, her voice soft, said, "No, Miguel. I'm not angry." She fought the impulse to run back into his arms, to feel his lips against hers once more, to be so close their hearts beat one against the other…

Miguel took a step toward her. She started to reach out to him, but then turned and headed back to camp. If not for the snow, she would have skipped. She said his name in her mind. *Miguel, Miguel!* Then she thought, *What about Nicolas?* And she didn't know whether to cry or shout for joy.

Later that day, a whispering snow fell. Fernanda, her brothers, and the other children danced around, trying to catch snowflakes in their hands or on their tongues. Antonio scooped up a handful of snow and threw it at Marcos. Other boys and girls joined in, their puffy breaths mingling with the falling snow.

Feathery snowflakes lighted on Fernanda's eyelashes and cheeks. She held out her arms and the frosty crystals drifted onto her upturned palms. Miguel was right. How could something so light and delicate contain such coldness? She hadn't seen Miguel since the morning, and wondered where he'd been all day. Her body tingled at the memory of his kiss, of his soft lips. How different his kiss had been from Nicolas's where she'd felt…nothing. She imagined kissing Miguel again…A snowball hitting her back knocked Miguel and Nicolas from her mind. Laughing, she scooped up a handful of snow and aimed for Antonio.

Luis ran up, calling, "The soldiers from the second division have arrived! They're weak and frozen, and many of the cattle have died."

Fernanda followed Luis to the returning soldiers. They limped into camp, some soldiers holding up others who were crippled from the storm. Others slumped forward on the saddles of scraggy horses. After nearly two weeks of fighting snow and wind and ice, their uniforms hung loose on their gaunt bodies.

"Fifteen saddle animals are either lost or dead," one soldier said in a raspy voice.

Sergeant Grijalba helped a soldier, his face as gray as the sky, from his horse. "The storm caught us on the road. We decided to march forward instead of taking the chance of being trapped in more severe conditions." The sergeant coughed and briefly leaned against the horse. "Thank God we didn't lose any men. But Aquino," he nodded at the sick soldier. "I fear for his health. We need blankets and a fire. Is there a tent we can take him to?"

This dying soldier could be Nicolas, Fernanda thought. Where was he? Was he safe? "There are no soldiers' barracks here," she said. "Only families. You may bring him to our tent. We have room and enough blankets."

Fernanda led the soldiers, asking people to gather wood and bring it to the tent. As she approached the tent, she saw Miguel stacking wood near the opening.

"I've brought you wood for the night," he said. And though his face was impassive, his eyes were bright with desire as he gazed at Fernanda.

Fernanda saw how he struggled to keep his face impassive; still, his eyes couldn't hide his desire for her. She wanted so much to go to him, to be in his arms again, but she kept her face a neutral mask. "Thank you. We need the wood for this poor soldier," she said. Her focus returned to the returning soldiers. "You should see them all, Miguel. They're ravaged from the snow storm." She opened the tent flap. "Take him in," she told the soldiers.

As the soldiers carried the sick man past Miguel, his mouth twisted, and Fernanda realized he reacted to all soldiers in the same way. They were no better than Apaches he'd said at Casa Grande. Why did he think that?

She gestured at the soldier. "Miguel…" How could he be cruel to such a sick man?

The anger in Miguel's eyes had returned, but they were also full of anguish. "You don't understand…it's what they did…" He glared at the soldiers' backs as they disappeared into the tent. "I can't—" And then, his hands clenched at his sides, he stomped away.

Fernanda started to call him back, but the other soldiers came out of the tent, and she went inside. Luis had built up a fire, and as Fernanda wrapped blankets around the prostrate soldier, she worried about Nicolas, hoping he was safe and wondering when he would return. She thought about Miguel, what he had meant, what it was that she didn't understand. Would he or Gloria ever tell her? Then she thought again of Nicolas, and the knot of worry in her stomach tightened.

She stayed at the soldier's side. The tent heated up, and Fernanda wiped her hand across her sweating upper lip. She hadn't been so warm for weeks. Slowly, color returned to the soldier's face, and within a few hours, he was talking and sipping water.

Two days later, as Fernanda collected wood, a horse straggled into camp carrying a stiff shivering soldier. She ran to him, saw other soldiers following, and shouted back to the camp, "The third division! Please help, the third division has arrived."

Lieutenant Moraga rode up as other campers rushed to help.

"Are all the men here?" Fernanda asked, looking at each soldier.

The lieutenant said, "I can't hear very well. The cold, so painful. We were caught in the severest part of the storm, but we continued to march rather than be buried in the snow. My men need water and warmth. Some are frozen and, I fear, close to death."

Another horse trailed into camp, stumbling, even though the emaciated soldier it carried couldn't have been a heavy burden. Then Fernanda saw it was Nicolas. She rushed to him and gasped at the sight of his pale face, cracked lips, and stiff limbs. *Oh, God, please don't let him die.* She grabbed the reins and quickly led the horse to her tent. Nicolas groaned, but he didn't seem to recognize her.

Her family, Feliciana, and others came and went, but Fernanda never left Nicolas's side. She kept the fire going and blankets tucked around him. As the hours passed, he remained unconscious.

Alone in the tent, she cried while rubbing Nicolas's hands and laying her palms on his cold face. What if he didn't get well? Oh, God, what if he should die? She wept. Nicolas had loved her, cared for her, and all she'd done was treat him poorly. Touching his face, watching his shallow breathing, she prayed, *Please, God, please let him live.* She promised she would…she would…

A sudden realization struck her like a blast of frosty air. Nicolas, such a good man and a dear friend. But that's what she felt for him: the compassion and love she would for a beloved friend. She didn't love him as a wife should love her husband. She closed her eyes against a wave of dizziness. No, she didn't love him, and never had.

"Nicolas," she whispered. "I'm so sorry. Nicolas, please get well. Please." Her eyes burned from weeping. She wanted to cry again, to have that relief, but she had shed all her tears.

There was a stirring behind her, and someone entered the tent. "Fernanda," Miguel said quietly.

Her sorrow for Nicolas couldn't keep her heart from skipping at the sound of Miguel's voice. "Come in," she said.

"How is he?" Miguel asked.

She placed her hand on Nicolas's shoulder. "He hasn't regained consciousness."

"He'll be fine. The other soldiers are slowly recovering."

His manner, his complete lack of sympathy, made her catch her breath. How could he be so caring and gentle one moment, and then act as cold as the snow that covered the ground? Was he jealous of Nicolas? Fernanda's face burned. They hadn't had a chance to speak further after their kiss. To speak of any feelings between them. But she knew they both felt…something. Even now, as her anger and confusion grew, his closeness spread a warmth through her body that made her want to feel his touch as she had at Casa Grande, at the fandango, at the well. But what was the fury he carried inside that stomped out his other, loving self?

She stood and whispered fiercely, "I know you and Nicolas don't like each other. But it's not just him. It's all soldiers. Why, Miguel? Why such anger, such hatred? What is it? What?"

Miguel's jaw stiffened, and he turned as if to leave.

"You seem to be two different people, Miguel." Fernanda softened her tone. "I–I care about you—" he froze "—and–and Gloria. I want to understand."

Miguel hesitated. Then he swung around. "Fine. I'll tell you. I'll tell you my story." He slapped his chest. "*My* sad story that I wish to forget but can't because I'm surrounded by reminders—" He jerked his hand at Nicolas "—every day." He began pacing around the tent. "Like your parents, my father was Spanish, my mother Indian, a Papago. Both my parents wanted to be known as Spaniards, and they taught Gloria and me nothing about the Papagos. When I grew older, I wanted to know more about my ancestry. I became friendly with a nearby village of Papagos, learning their language, their traditions. Later, I fell in—I met a young woman, Hahth. We—" he choked and swallowed "—we wanted to marry."

Fernanda breathed in sharply. He–he was in love with another? They were married? She twisted the material of her skirt around her fingers.

Miguel continued. "Of course, I wanted my parents' blessing, and I finally convinced them to come to the village with me. We shared food with Hahth and her family. I thought things were going well. Then—" Miguel's jaw muscles worked as he clenched his teeth. "Then three or four young Papago men galloped into the village. They shouted that soldiers were coming, angry soldiers. There was danger."

Fernanda swung her head back to Miguel, her jealousy forgotten.

Miguel rushed his words as if he couldn't bear to keep them in his mouth. "The villagers scattered, screaming. Soldiers charged into the village, shouting something about horse thieves." He rubbed his hand across his face and moaned. "By the time they passed through the village, many of the people were dead, mostly young men, but women, too. Including my parents and Hahth." Miguel pounded his fists on his thighs. "Dead! Little children left orphaned, crying, screaming for their parents, seeing them lying there broken and bleeding!"

"Miguel," Fernanda whispered. "I'm so sorry. Why? Why did the soldiers kill the villagers? Why did they kill your parents?"

Miguel paced again, his hands clenched into fists. "There was much confusion with people running and screaming. As the soldiers swung their swords, they shouted, 'Apache horse thieves!' But nobody there was Apache, and no one had stolen horses. A soldier attacked me." He touched the scar on his face. "I fought him off, only wanting to get everyone—my parents, Hahth and her family—to safety. I lost sight of them.

Later, I found them, but by then, it–it was too late. They were dead."

"Oh my God! What of Gloria? Was she there? Did she see your parents die?"

"No, thank God. They had insisted she stay at home." He grasped his forehead, swaying slightly. "What if she'd been there? What if…?

Fernanda cried into her hands. So horrible. Poor Miguel. Poor Gloria. She wanted to go back to the time before this terrible journey. Why did they come? Why did Mama die? How she wished Mama were here! She stumbled to Miguel and grasped his hand. "I'm sorry, Miguel. I'm so sorry."

Miguel stood over Nicolas, his lip curling as if he would spit on him, or worse. "Now you understand my hatred of the Spanish soldiers."

She wiped her eyes as his words penetrated her shock. "But Miguel, Nicolas didn't kill your parents."

"They're all the same. War and killing are all they know." His eyes blazed, wet with tears. "I don't understand how you can love him. A soldier's wife? No, Fernanda, that can't be *your* life."

Fernanda stepped back. His lack of compassion. His blind hatred of all soldiers. And now, telling her what was right for her. "You can't tell me what my life can or can't be. Don't think you know so much about me." She glanced at Nicolas who remained asleep, and she lowered her voice, still tense. "I told you our marriage wasn't decided, but now it is. Even though after this terrible illness it'll be cruel and heartless to tell him, I won't marry him. I won't marry at all. I never wanted to marry, and that's as true now as it ever was. Why can't everyone simply leave me alone? I just want to be left alone!" Her voice had risen, and now she ran back to Nicolas, afraid that she'd disturbed him, but he hadn't stirred.

She knelt down at his side, draped her arms across his chest, and cried.

Miguel, who'd walked to the tent opening, turned back and said, his voice now gentle, "You told me once, Fernanda, when we first met, that I was wrong to isolate myself from others. Now I'm telling you that love, and marriage, with– with the right person, doesn't have to be a prison."

To Fernanda, sick with anger, sorrow, and confusion, his words were meaningless, and she said nothing. Miguel started to speak again, but the words caught in his throat, and he left the tent.

Chapter Fifteen

December 20-25, 1775

Papa, his shoulders hunched from the cold, shuffled up to Fernanda and her brothers where they huddled together outside the tent. "Fifty cattle are dead," he said.

"So many?" Fernanda said.

"They were weak and didn't survive the freezing overnight temperatures. Three more horses are also gone. One of them is Miguel's."

Oh, his beautiful horse. Beautiful, at least, until the journey ravaged it. And two other horses dead, meaning more people without mounts, more people walking in the snow. Already, she and her family shared only Aletta and one horse. They had all slumped into a heavy lethargy. Had their hopes been buried with the dead animals? Their dreams lost in the flurry of wind and rain and snow? She lifted Ignacio, and then peered up at the mountains towering over them. Later that day, they would start the ascent. She held her brother close. For his sake, for all their sakes, she had to hold onto the promise of California.

As she packed the family's belongings into the trunk, Fernanda rolled her head on her neck, trying to relieve the knot between her shoulder blades. Thank God Nicolas and the other soldiers had recovered. For that she could be thankful. Now she had to speak to Nicolas and tell him she couldn't marry him. How would she explain that she didn't love him? That if they married, they'd both be miserable. He wanting her to act a certain way, she constantly fighting his demands. *Get riding out of your system*, he'd said at the Yuma horse race. *You were born to ride*, Miguel had said. She closed the trunk and sighed. As for Miguel…She hadn't spoken to him since he told his tragic story and left her with Nicolas, almost one week before.

Outside the tent, she said to Papa, "I'll return shortly."

"We'll be leaving soon, Mi'ja."

Fernanda, forcing each heavy dragging step, found Nicolas with the other soldiers saddling his horse. As she approached, her stomach tightened as if she, too, had a saddle cinched around her middle. "Nicolas, can I see you alone?"

Nicolas nodded, finished securing the saddle, and guided Fernanda away from the other soldiers. She could see he tried to walk straight in his soldierly fashion, but his shoulders sagged and his back curved slightly. Yes, he had recovered, his manner still proud, but he was weakened. The journey was changing them all.

"Nicolas, I–I haven't been honest with you, or myself."

"And how is that, Fernanda?" Nicolas asked quietly.

"I can't…It wouldn't be right for me to accept your proposal of marriage." She put her hand on his arm. "Oh, Nicolas, can you forgive me?"

He stared at her. Then he narrowed his eyes. Stepping backward, he jerked his arm from her touch. "Forgive you? Forgive you for all the months that you kept me waiting?

Forgive you for all the times you told me, 'Soon, Nicolas, soon'? I've been a fool. An imbecile. I knew this was coming, but I refused to face it because I love you. Forgive you? No, I won't forgive you!" He turned his back to her, his fists tight at his side. A moment later, he swung around to face her. "I know who stands behind all this." He spat on the ground. "It's that yellow dog, that spineless coward, isn't it? For weeks, I've watched how he lurks around you, how his eyes follow you."

"That's not true." But even now, she had no control over the pleasure that coursed through her at the thought of Miguel. "Nicolas, I—" She reached to touch his arm again, but when he stiffened, she dropped her hand. "I'm sorry. Truly. I didn't mean to deceive you. Please try to understand. I was so confused about our marriage, if it was the right thing for me, for us. I was searching for something, wanting something else. A different kind of life than my mother's."

Nicolas sneered, startling Fernanda with its ugliness. "A different kind of life? What might that be? Your mother led a proud life. I'm sure she'd tell you that she had been happy."

"That's not what I'm saying. You're twisting my words. I mean…what I'm trying to say…Oh, you just don't understand. I want to decide, to choose, what's right for me."

"You're right, I don't understand. You've changed. I understood you when you were a young girl—"

"But I *haven't* changed. Don't you see that's the problem? It was fine for me then to be the precocious one, the adventurous one. Now everyone *wants* me to change. Prim, proper, the perfect lady. Well, I'm not a perfect lady, and I never will be."

"No, you won't!"

Fernanda, shocked, said nothing.

Slowly, the fury relaxed from Nicolas's face. "It's true, Fernanda, you were an impetuous child, and I indulged you.

When you became a woman, I did want you to act a certain way. But things have changed. I've changed. I won't treat you that way anymore."

He seemed so sincere, but she knew in time their life would fall into the routine of military life. He *would* have certain expectations of her. Expectations she wouldn't be able to fulfill.

Nicolas took her hand between his two. "I do love you. I can give you a good life, security."

She didn't want to marry simply for security. "I love you, Nicolas. But not in the way you wish. You must believe I'm doing the right thing, for us both."

Nicolas dropped her hand. "I don't believe you're doing the right thing. But apparently I won't change your mind." His face and lips were pale. "I hope you don't live to regret this, Fernanda."

Hurt shadowed his eyes, but Fernanda saw other emotions that mirrored her own: sadness and regret, memories of the past, speculation about the future. Such twists and turns life presented. People take different paths, sometimes knowingly, sometimes not. A turn here, a turn there, and your life is changed forever.

Later that day, the colonists threaded their way through a narrow mountain pass that had captured the coldest of the icy air. Though Fernanda's fingers and toes seemed numb and lifeless, they ached with a raw pain. "At least there's no snow," she muttered.

"Wh–what, Nanda?" Ignacio's teeth chattered.

"Nothing, sweet brother. Just think of the warm fire we'll have later."

And soon after, Captain Anza called for them to halt in a dry gully not far from a meager spring. While Papa, Luis, and Antonio set up the tent, Fernanda took the other boys and Tomása with her to collect wood. Fernanda gave Ignacio and Tomása the important job of gathering kindling. They had almost as much as they could carry and were about to turn back, when two Indian women appeared above them, each carrying a basket. The colonists had passed through a few small villages, and the Indians either fled or stayed hidden, so it was a surprise to see these women so close. The children stared up at them, and the women froze like deer confronted by hunters. They dropped their baskets and scurried back up the mountain.

"Let's see what's in their baskets," Marcos said, and he and Jorge ran ahead. Fernanda followed, holding Ignacio's and Tomása's hands. The two boys peered into the baskets, and their faces drooped with disappointment.

"No dead rabbits," Jorge said.

"Just some seeds and berries," Fernanda said. "Such scant bits of food. We'll leave them here. I'm sure the women will return once we're gone."

On the way back to camp, Fernanda decided to share some of their food with the Indians. When they returned to camp, she raced to her tent, scooped some beans into her bundled rebozo, and ran back to where the women had been. She tiptoed up the slope and dropped a few handfuls of beans into each basket.

She gazed up the mountain, hoping the women would return before dark. Just as she turned to go, a movement caught her eye. It was Miguel, making his way up the rocky hillside. She stopped herself from calling out his name. Why was he heading in the direction of the village? A hot flame of jealousy seared her lungs as she wondered if he'd found another woman to care for. She tried to tell herself it didn't matter to her. But, watching Miguel's retreating figure, an empty feeling overcame her, and she headed back to camp.

The following morning, Fernanda woke and rubbed her eyes. Oh, it was so cold. She burrowed under her blanket, snuggled closer to Ignacio, and whispered, "Wake up, little brother. It's Christmas."

Ignacio's eyes widened. "I forgot." He hopped up from the bedroll and clapped his hands. "Piñata!" Small white clouds puffed from his mouth.

"No piñata today, Nacio." No lighted candles, or ringing mission bells, or sugared cakes fried in fat. "But we can still celebrate." Before Fernanda left the tent, she pulled out her new rebozo, thinking that was one way she could make the day special.

Outside, gray clouds covered the sky, and patches of fog hovered here and there around the campsite. Feliciana and Micaela already had the fire blazing.

"*Feliz Navidad,*" Fernanda said.

"Merry Christmas," the women replied.

Micaela said, "Captain Anza distributed an extra ration of chocolate for the holiday. We can have hot cocoa with our breakfast."

Tomása had come out of her tent, and she and Ignacio held hands, dancing about shouting, "Choc'late. Feliz Navidad!"

"Not only that, *niños,*" Feliciana said. "Cinnamon and sugar to sprinkle on our tortillas. What a feast we'll have this morning."

Soon they were all sitting around the fire, savoring each sip of cocoa, each bite of the sweetened tortillas. Across the circle, Miguel kept eyeing her, then, when she looked his way, darting his eyes in another direction. Fernanda could see the tension in his entire body. His shoulders were hunched, his fingertips white as he clenched his cup of cooca, all as if he concealed some secret. Was it about the woman he'd visited up the mountain? As she drank the last drop of her cocoa, some of her joy drained away with it.

After she helped clean up, Fernanda walked back to the tent. Footsteps pounded behind her, and there was Miguel, shuffling at her side, saying, "Feliz Navidad."

"Feliz Navidad," Fernanda murmured.

"It was a delicious breakfast, no?" Miguel looked at the ground, at the trees, anywhere except Fernanda.

"Yes, delicious."

Miguel touched her arm. "Fernanda, please stop for a moment. I know you're angry with me. I–I've thought much about that night, and what you said."

He cupped her elbow, leading her away from camp. Glancing back at her tent, Fernanda saw Ignacio safely with his brothers, so she walked with Miguel.

She couldn't deny the feeling his presence gave her, how her heart beat a little faster, pulsing in her neck, spreading warmth to her chest and her face.

But why was he so nervous?

"First," he said, "there's something I must explain."

Here it comes, Fernanda thought. Picturing him with another woman, her legs suddenly felt heavy as if she wore iron skillets for shoes, and she stopped walking.

"I have—I had such fury inside me after Hahth and my parents died," Miguel continued. "I needed someone to blame, so I blamed *all* soldiers for their deaths."

Fernanda lifted her head, listening more closely to his words.

"You see, I–I didn't tell you everything. The soldiers hadn't been ordered to raid the village, and their superiors punished them. I'm sorry I lied to you."

"Miguel, you lost your parents and–and Hahth. I can understand your anger."

"Yes, when it happened. But later, I didn't handle it well. I hurt others, including my sister. I was a coward." His eyes showed disgust, obviously with himself.

"Don't speak that way. You suffered a horrible tragedy."

"I only wish I was as brave as you."

"Me? I am not brave! And look at the courage it took for you to tell me what really happened." She turned her face away from Miguel's. "No, I'm not brave. I've held a secret inside, too, but it's worse, much worse."

"You can trust me, Fernanda," Miguel said gently.

"It–it happened the day before my mother died." A damp coldness invaded her body. She felt ill and weak as she remembered that day. If she told, she'd surely be sick. And what would Miguel think of her bravery then?

"What happened?" he asked, his voice still soft.

"My mother and I had a terrible fight. I went to bed angry, refusing to speak to her. Then that–that last morning, she was so nice to me, and I—" she spoke through her tears "—I let her leave without giving her a smile, without speaking a kind word. I'll never, ever be able to fix that."

"You must believe your mother knew how much you loved her."

"Yes, I do believe that. But there are so many things I should have said to Mama. There's so much I should have learned about her. Now it's too late."

Miguel clutched her hands. "Listen. This is what else I wanted to tell you. I believe I found someone who knows the story of your mother and great-grandmother."

For one second, Fernanda stopped breathing. Miguel's words roared through her head. He tightened his grasp on her hands as she stumbled backward. "What? What did you say?"

"I went up the mountain yesterday and found a village. An old woman lives there. She's Pima. She must have come here years ago, perhaps married into this tribe. She speaks the Pima language clearly. I can take you to her if you will come."

"Yes, please," Fernanda said, dizzy with disbelief and hope. "Please take me."

Chapter Sixteen

December 25, 1775

Fernanda followed Miguel past the rocks where the Indian women had dropped their baskets. As they climbed, the slope got steeper.

Miguel offered her his hand. "Come."

Her dream. Again! And there truly was an old woman awaiting her on top of the mountain. Not her great-grandmother as she had suspected, but another woman who might know the truth about her mother's past. She grabbed Miguel's hand. He pulled her up onto a boulder, and then they hopped down onto a path that wound farther up the mountain.

"It's easy from here," Miguel said. "Just a short distance."

They walked on, and Fernanda stared straight ahead, watching for the first sign of the village. What if the woman didn't know her mother after all? What if she did? What if it were true that Great-grandmother *had* abandoned Mama in the desert?

Miguel pointed ahead. "There's the village."

Fernanda breathed deeply, but she couldn't unravel the knot in her stomach. She followed Miguel into a meadow dotted with four huts similar to those of the Pimas and Yumas. They walked past a family—a woman building a fire, a man skinning a rabbit, and two children chasing each other around the boulders and bushes. The children stopped their game to stare at the strangers. Miguel nodded at the adults. They eyed Fernanda then returned to their work.

Miguel stopped near the small door of a hut and called out in the Pima language. A woman's shaky voice answered. Miguel squatted, waved to Fernanda, and they crawled through the blanket-covered opening.

A small pile of red coals smoldered in the center of the round hut. Light filtered through the sides of the brush walls. As Fernanda's eyes adjusted to the shadowy interior, she saw the old woman lying on a blanket cushioned with leaves. Like the old woman in the dream, her loose white hair streamed over her shoulders and across the blanket. She motioned her hand limply toward the floor, indicating they should sit. Fernanda and Miguel sat on the dirt floor, facing her across the fire.

The woman pushed herself up, sat cross-legged, and pulled the frayed blanket around her legs. She tugged another blanket over the grass shawl that covered her shoulders and breasts. Miguel spoke to her, and Fernanda recognized her mother's Pima name, Heosig, and her great-grandmother's name, Suhna. He gestured toward Fernanda, and the old woman gazed at her as if she could see into her mind and deep into her very soul. Fernanda rubbed her arms and inched closer to the coals.

"You may address her as Sikul—great-great-grand-mother—if you wish," Miguel told Fernanda.

Then Sikul began to speak.

She kept her eyes on Fernanda, and when Miguel interpreted, Fernanda understood that Sikul addressed her directly.

The old woman's gentle voice and the musical sounds of the Pima language enveloped Fernanda, and she felt as if she and Sikul were alone in the dusky hut.

"At the time when your mother, Heosig, was a small girl, she, her mother Marsatû, and many of our people lived at the mission among the Black Robes. Heosig was known by Pimas throughout the area not only for the mystery of the flower on her face, but for her beauty, kind spirit, and diligence. Even at an early age, she won many hearts."

Fernanda held her arms close to her waist, hugging the excitement that rippled through her body.

"We went to the mission," Sikul said, "for protection against Apache warriors, for livestock and meat, for seeds and the land to cultivate them. We learned to use their plows and hoes, their sickles and saws. Some chose to live in the *olas-ki* of our ancestors, and built the round huts near the mission. But others, heeding the priests' wishes that we live like the white man, built adobe dwellings and wore the trousers and petticoats the priests gave us."

Fernanda imagined Mama at the mission, a young Pima girl uncomfortable in her new confining clothes, just as Captain Palma had tugged at the soldier's uniform.

Sikul went on. "For all this, the Black Robes asked for nothing in return except that we learn about their god, their heaven and hell, their Christianity. We were in awe of their god's power and the Black Robes' ceremonies. Some of our men were given scepters with silver knobs and flowing ribbons. Although they had no authority with the Pimas, it was through these men that the priests administered their laws." Sikul's blanket slipped. With knobby, thick-veined hands, she tugged it back over her shoulders then continued.

"The Black Robes enticed our children with gifts their mothers and fathers couldn't give. Parents went to the mission to claim back their children. Once there, many decided to stay."

That must be what Papa meant when he spoke of ploys, Fernanda thought.

"There were those," Sikul said, "who didn't want to follow the ways of the Black Robes' god. They lived their lives as the Pimas had always lived, under the eyes of the gods Elder Brother and Earth Doctor. Your great-grandmother, Suhna, was one of those. Even though it meant she wouldn't be with Heosig and Marsatû, she refused to live at the mission or to accept the priest's god."

Fernanda clasped her hands tightly in her lap at the mention of her great-grandmother's name. Now she would learn the truth.

"Some days," Sikul continued, "Suhna came to the mission to visit, and other days she brought Heosig to the village to teach her Pima songs and other traditions. In this way, your mother split her heart between two worlds: the mission and the Pima village.

"As time went on, some at the mission became discontented. They began to denounce the priests, the soldiers, the white man's leaders. We were being mistreated, they said. We were the Black Robes' slaves, they told us. We at the mission listened with our ears and then with our hearts. Yes, some things they said were true. We were forced to plant the fields even when we didn't want to. Children were dying from the white man's diseases. Women and men were being punished with lashings. Sons lost respect for their fathers who were forced to do women's work."

Fernanda's mind buzzed with confusion at Sikul's words. The missions were helpful to the Indians, weren't they? They provided food and protection. Her mother had never said a bad word about the missions or the priests.

"And one day…" Sikul raised her voice, as if to interrupt Fernanda's thoughts. "And one day, we rose up against the Black Robes." The coals on the fire shifted. The old woman continued, her voice raspy. "There was a terrible war. Blood covered the land, flowing from the jagged wounds of musket shots and the piercings of a thousand arrows."

Fernanda dug her fingers into her thighs.

"Black Robes died. White people died. Pimas died. Marsatû died."

Harder, harder Fernanda gripped her legs, pressing deep into her muscles, hoping, somehow, the pain might keep her from feeling the horror of Sikul's story. Poor Mama, her father already dead at the hands of the Apaches, and now her mother also killed so brutally. But…what about the Apaches? "Miguel, ask her about the Apaches. Mama told us her mother was killed by Apaches. Were they there?"

Miguel questioned Sikul then reached for Fernanda's hand and said gently, "No Apaches fought at the mission. Just Pimas and soldiers. The priests must have told your mother that Apaches killed Marsatû."

Fernanda's mind flashed with images of the soldiers on the expedition, of their muskets and ten-foot-long lances, of Nicolas gripping his sword…Her friends. Her neighbors. They had killed her grandmother. How could they?

Wait. What was she thinking? Of course those soldiers hadn't killed Grandmother. She moaned. She'd been so angry with Miguel for blaming all soldiers for his parents' and Hahth's deaths. Now she was doing the same. She dropped her head into her hands and silently cried.

Sikul was still talking. "New white rulers signed a treaty with our leaders, and we returned to the mission. The Black Robes took Heosig in with the other orphans. Suhna came to claim her—" The old woman hacked and clutched the blanket around her throat. "—came to claim Heosig to raise her as a true Pima. The priests refused to let her go. So Suhna devised a plan, and on a dark moonless night, she stole your mother away."

Fernanda jerked her head up, all her attention now on Sikul.

"The Black Robes, with the help of the soldiers, found Heosig and brought her back to the mission. All we knew is what the priests told us: the heathen Suhna had abandoned your mother in the desert. And that's what young Heosig was brought up to believe."

Fernanda's body tensed, and she leaned toward the old woman. *It's not true*, she wanted to shout. *Tell me it's not true.*

"Time passed." Sikul's voice had lowered. "Like all of us at the mission, Heosig lived her life under the influence of the Black Robes. Each day carried us further away from our Pima traditions. Then one day, a white man came to the mission. Love grew between him and Heosig. He took her away to be his wife. That's all I know of your mother." The hand that clenched the blanket at her throat shook, and she closed her eyes.

Fernanda stared at the pile of coals, now covered in a layer of ash. The room had dimmed and cooled without their warmth. Her head throbbed with the weight of her disappointment. So, it was true after all. Great-grandmother had left Mama, alone, afraid, in the desert. What Fernanda had felt inside, about her mother and great-grandmother, were those all lies? She couldn't trust her deepest feelings? She dropped her chin to her hollow, aching chest. Now what would she do?

Miguel touched her knee. "Fernanda, are you listening?"

Sikul's gravelly voice had continued. "As for Suhna—"

Fernanda slowly raised her head.

"—we hadn't seen her for many years. She suddenly appeared at the time of the saguaro harvest festival. She wished to bring Heosig to the village celebration. When Suhna learned that your mother was gone, that we couldn't tell her where she now lived, her face withered and dried before our eyes like the molted skin of a snake. We asked her about the time she stole Heosig, and if it were true she had abandoned her in the desert. Suhna's eyes sparked, and she told us what the Black Robes had not: that the priests and soldiers had ridden into the village and demanded the return of Heosig. Suhna refused. The chief and village council, to avoid confrontation with the Spanish soldiers, forced Suhna to let your mother go. The priests and the council forbade her to visit Heosig, and that's why she stayed away those many years. After Suhna told us this story, she returned to the village. We watched her ride away with Sorrow as her dark companion, her back surrendering to its weight. That's the last we saw of your great-grandmother. I believe her soul has gone to Morning Base."

Fernanda raised her hand to her lips. All those years Mama had renounced her Pima past. All those years she believed a horrible lie about her beloved grandmother. Oh, if only she could tell Mama what she knew. That Great-grandmother truly loved her. That she didn't desert her. That she came back for her.

But then Fernanda closed her eyes and a smile spread through her. Mama *did* know, for surely she and Great-grandmother were reunited. And Fernanda had given Mama the gift she had promised her that night before the journey began. A gift to Mama *and* Great-grandmother, a gift of truth so they could have peace and love between them—forever.

Fernanda said to Sikul, "Thank you. I thank you with all my heart for this knowledge."

Sikul nodded. There was no need for Miguel to translate.

"I—I have one more favor to ask, if I may," Fernanda said. "I'd like to know my name as it's spoken in the Pima language."

"Your name can't be directly translated," Miguel said. "The Pimas take their names from something they like. For instance flower, sky, river."

"Oh." Fernanda played with the end of her braid. Of course! She'd pick "horse" for her name. Then she remembered how her mother's face would light up whenever she saw the colorful moths at night or the butterflies during the day. Yes, butterflies were light and free and beautiful, and they had made her mother smile. "Butterfly. Please tell Sikul I'd like my Pima name to be Butterfly."

When Miguel translated, Sikul nodded and said, "Yâkimali."

"Yâkimali," Fernanda repeated. Then slowly, enjoying how her mouth formed the word. "Yâkimali."

They stood to leave. Miguel placed some wood on the coals, and soon orange flames flickered around the small logs.

Fernanda said, "Oh, we should give her something. To thank her."

Miguel looked around, as if hoping to find some gift lying on the ground. "We have nothing to give her."

His words echoed her own the night Aqwaq had given her the necklace. She fingered the shell at her neck. She'd told herself she had nothing to give in return. But she did that night, and she did now. Her new rebozo. Her beautiful rebozo with its fine embroidery and golden fringe. Her rebozo that she should have given to Aqwaq. What better gift to present to this woman who had given her the truth about Mama and Great-grandmother. "Yes, Miguel, we have something for Sikul." She walked around the fire and, squatting next to the old woman, slipped the shawl from her shoulders and wrapped it around Sikul.

Sikul stroked it with her gnarled hands. Then she rested her palm, dry and rough like a piece of bark, against Fernanda's cheek. "Yâkimali." Her voice was hoarse from her storytelling. She uttered more words, and Miguel translated.

"I see the spirits of Suhna and Heosig live in your soul. Because you sought the truth, their journey has finally ended. For you, another begins. May Elder Brother and Earth Doctor guide you on your new journey."

Mama and Great-grandmother lived inside her, and she had somehow helped them! There was nothing, nothing, anyone could have said that would fill Fernanda with such happiness. As if joy were a thing she could hold in her arms. And she'd hold those words, that joy, close to her heart for the rest of her life.

Fernanda and Miguel followed the trail out of the village. Sikul's words whirled through her head. She didn't want to forget one detail the old woman had told her. "Miguel, can we stop for a moment? I must think, there's so much to understand."

"We can sit on this boulder."

When they sat, their legs couldn't help but touch. Fernanda stared straight ahead, trying to slow her heart as she remembered Miguel's kiss. Then she secretly glanced at him. His head was bent, strands of hair falling forward. She had an urge to brush the hair away from his face, and as if reading her mind, he pushed it back, keeping his hand in his hair and turning to her—the gesture she loved.

He smiled at her, and shyly, briefly, she touched his arm. "Thank you. I can't tell you how much this means to me, to learn the truth about my mother and great-grandmother. Poor Mama. I wish she'd known what truly happened. But they're together now. Do you know what this Morning Base is Sikul spoke of?"

"The Pimas believe that after death all souls go to Morning Base, the place where the sun rises. They don't believe in a heaven or hell, reward or punishment. At Morning Base, they celebrate with dancing and feasting. They enter that world wearing their finest clothing."

Fernanda pictured her mother and great-grandmother together in the sun-filled Morning Base, wearing silk rebozos rich with embroidery, feasting on juicy meats and sweet creamy chocolate. "Oh, I like the idea of Morning Base. Similar to Heaven. How wonderful they have no hell. But confusing. Do they believe even bad people go to Morning Base?"

Miguel shrugged. "I don't really know. Perhaps they believe no one is truly bad."

"Even the soldiers who killed your parents, and Hahth, and my grandmother?"

"Perhaps the Pimas believe peoples' souls aren't evil, that the evil is in the time and place and circumstances."

"And what about the circumstances at the mission? Mama never said a bad word about the mission, but something went terribly wrong. Do you think the priests were to blame? The soldiers? The governor?" At Casa Grande, Miguel had helped Fernanda see the Indians from their perspective when he and Luis had argued about the soldiers and Apaches. Feliciana had done the same when she said Indians and Spaniards had their own way of dressing, their own customs. "Perhaps the Pimas shouldn't have come to the mission in the first place, forced to live as we do."

"Ay, I don't know," Miguel said. "Why is it better to live the Spanish way? Why is it better to be called Spaniard? Why are people given names depending on how big their drop of Spanish blood is, mestizo, castizo, coyote, mulatto?"

"It's true. My mother, your parents, all people want to be known as Spaniards. They will claim it if they can get away with it. But why should it matter?"

"The answer is, it shouldn't. I'm tired of those prejudices and tired of all the fighting." He glanced at her. "Believe me, I really am. And it's not just one group who's to blame. Apaches killed your grandfather. Soldiers killed your grandmother, my parents, Hahth. Pimas killed soldiers and priests." Miguel bowed his head, holding it between his hands. "I don't want to live a life with killing, always killing."

"Miguel, that's in the past. We don't have to think about it now." Fernanda was sorry she had reminded Miguel of his pain. But she felt such ease talking to him, sorting out the confusing questions that cluttered her mind. "I loved hearing Sikul talk about my mother and great-grandmother. Great-grandmother sounded like a person who wanted to do things her own way. Once, Mama said I was like her. I suppose that's what she meant."

"Your great-grandmother fought for those she loved. That's the quality your mother must have also seen in you, Fernanda."

"I wish it were true. But–but I'm afraid that for my entire life I've only thought of myself." *Instead of helping Mama, instead of being honest with Nicolas...* "I didn't realize how selfish I've been until now, until this journey and all that's happened." Her face burned with her confession, but she also felt relief at saying it aloud.

Miguel took her hands in his. "Fernanda, didn't you hear Sikul say you have Heosig and Suhna's spirits inside you?

Who's the one who held your family together when your mother died? Who nurtured them on this journey? Who's the one who helped the Feliz children begin to accept their mother's death? Who stood by the women in labor, Nicolas and the other sick soldiers, the dying animals? You, Fernanda. You fight for the people and things you love. That's the spirit Sikul was talking about: the power and strength of your love."

Miguel's words swam in her head. She saw herself as weak, not strong, not thinking of others as she should, only wishing for her own enjoyment. How could what he said be true?

Miguel was still talking, breaking into her thoughts, confusing her even more.

"And that's what *I* saw in you, Fernanda. I watched how you cared for those around you. I watched how you kept their spirits up, never surrendering to fear or despair." He glanced away then stared at her with his dark eyes, now so open as if he no longer had secrets to conceal. "I thought I didn't need anyone else. Just Gloria. I thought I was protecting her, when I was actually hurting her, keeping her from others, keeping myself from the chance of more pain. You changed that for me. You are—" he seemed to search for the words "—so beautiful, so in love with life, so passionate about your beliefs, and you fight for those beliefs." He held her face between his hands. His voice softened. "I love you, Fernanda." He slid his hand down, cupped her chin, and traced her lips with his thumb. "I love you as much as anyone can possibly love."

His hands slipped to her arms, and he gently pulled her close. "*Te amo,*" he murmured. Then he kissed her softly on the lips.

For that moment, all that existed for Fernanda was the touch of Miguel's lips on hers, the feel of his body so close to hers. He'd said he loved her, and his words were a joy that rushed from her head to the very tips of her toes. She returned his kiss, pressing against him, wishing to feel his body close… closer. He caressed the back of her neck. His other hand slid down her back, and he pulled her tighter against his broad chest. His heart pounded against hers. His heat inflamed her body. He parted his lips slightly and she did the same; their kiss deepened, their mouths probing, tasting, urging. Nerves she never knew existed tingled. Her desire was a torch burning inside her, a fiery blaze flaming hotter and hotter, wanting, needing the oneness with Miguel that Feliciana had described. *Mi amor,* Fernanda thought. *My love!*

Miguel slowly pulled back, keeping Fernanda in his embrace. As if emerging from a world where nothing existed except Miguel's kiss, his body, Fernanda became aware of her surroundings—the whistle of a bird, the roughness of the rock she sat on, the cool air and faint rays of sun. Did her face have the same look of joy she saw on Miguel's? Surely it must. Her head felt as if it might float away. In her mind, she twirled and leaped.

"Miguel, I love you. I've known it in my heart for quite some time."

And Miguel loved *her*, not some idea of what a woman should be. He had never asked her to change. He had only encouraged her to be herself. With him, she could be the person she truly was.

Miguel stroked her cheek. "You're beautiful, Fernanda. My beautiful butterfly, my Yâkimali."

"Yâkimali," Fernanda repeated, closing her eyes briefly, savoring the name and Miguel's caress. "Do you have a Papago name, Miguel?"

"At the village I told you of—"

She grasped his thigh. "I'm sorry, I didn't mean to remind you."

"No, I can speak of it now. There are good memories, too." His eyes softened, as if even now recalling some happy moment.

Fernanda waited for the stab of jealousy for his past with Hahth, but it didn't come. No. Hahth had made him happy, so she was part of the goodness in him.

"They loved to hear me play my flute," Miguel said. "If I agreed, they would have me play for hours. So they called me Kuhutham, musician. I thought it a good name."

"Kuhutham," Fernanda repeated. "Yes, it's a strong name, and fitting since you play the flute with such feeling." Miguel still stroked her cheek, and she placed her hand over his. "Is there…is there a Pima word for love?"

"Yes, Yâkimali, there is. It's tachchutham." He kissed her lips. "Tachchutham."

"Tach…chu…tham," she whispered, returning his kiss. She rested her head against his chest, her mind clear, her body sinking, relaxing into his love. "What will you do once we reach California?"

"In Horcasitas, I helped my father run his ranchero, raising cattle. I sold everything after—before Gloria and I joined the expedition. Unlike most of the colonists, I won't settle at the mission. My plan, my dream is to have a ranchero of my own."

Fernanda wondered what the missions would be like in California. As Sikul described? That was a long time ago. Surely things had changed. "I imagine Papa won't want to live at the mission, either."

"What about you, Fernanda? What's your dream?"

"My dream is to do whatever I choose to do." She laughed and sat up. "The only problem is, I don't know what that is—yet. I'll help Papa with the boys, of course. Get their new lives settled. Then? I'll see what there is to see."

"Perhaps you can see my vision of life in California: family and friends, fiestas, cattle grazing on lush hillsides that overlook the ranchero, well-built fences, an adobe house and fine carved furniture, a garden." Miguel pulled her close and murmured into her hair, "Do you see it, Yâkimali? I could use a skilled horsewoman such as yourself."

Fernanda didn't reply, but she kissed him, all the while picturing herself galloping across green hills with Miguel at her side.

On the way back down the mountain, Miguel held Fernanda's hand until she broke free and ran ahead, laughing, prancing over the rocks, trying to keep up with her leaping heart, her soaring heart. Soaring as it did when she rode horses, and now, soaring with love.

Chapter Seventeen

Paradise Valley

January 1, 1776

As the heavy fog thinned into cloudy wisps, the figure of Papa leading Antonio and Marcos atop the horse appeared before Fernanda. In the clearing haze, the horse stepped confidently down the path. Aletta, following behind and carrying Fernanda, Ignacio, and Jorge, picked up the faster pace. The sky opened with patches of brilliant blue. Fernanda squinted against the brightness, her joy rising like the mist that left dewdrops glistening in the sunlight. They were finally descending the mountain, and today they would reach the valley floor. It was *Año Nuevo*, the first day of the new year; the first day of their new lives.

If only her mother were there. Since listening to Sikul's story, so many memories of Mama had returned to her. And when a bird flitted by, its feathers as blue as the sky, she remembered a story Mama had told her when she was young, a Pima legend about bluebirds and coyotes. She understood now why Mama stopped telling the Pima tales: so they wouldn't ask questions about her Pima past. But their Pima ancestry shouldn't be forgotten, just as Great-grandmother wished. Now that Fernanda knew the truth, she was sure

Mama would have wanted it, too. She'd tell her brothers the Pima traditions she remembered. Someday they would tell their children, their children would pass them on, and each generation would know about the rich mixture of blood that flowed through their veins.

"Little Brothers," she said. "I was thinking of a Pima legend Mama told me when I was a little girl. Would you like to hear it?"

"Si!" Ignacio said.

"The legend tells us that the bluebird was once a very ugly color. The unfortunate bird decided to bathe in a lake four times every morning for four mornings. The bird sang this song while it bathed: 'There's a blue water. It lies there. I went in. I'm all blue.' On the fourth morning, the bird lost all its feathers. On the fifth morning it bathed once more and came out with blue feathers."

"And it stayed blue forever?" Jorge asked.

"Yes," Fernanda said. "But there's more. All the while that the bird bathed, Coyote watched. When he saw the beautiful bluebird, he was jealous and decided he wanted to be blue, too. At that time, Coyote was bright green."

The boys giggled.

"Coyote bathed in the lake four times for four days while singing the song, and on the fifth day he came out of the water as beautifully blue as the bird. He couldn't be more proud of his new color. In fact, he was so proud that as he walked along the road, he looked to the left to see if anyone noticed him. He looked to the right to see if anyone was admiring him. He even looked behind him to see if his shadow was blue. And since he wasn't watching the road, he fell across a stump and into the dirt. The dust covered up the lovely blue, and that's why, today, coyotes are the color of dirt."

"I like green coyote," Ignacio said.

Fernanda ruffled his hair. She vowed to try to remember more of Mama's stories, and learn as much about the Pimas as she could.

Ahead, voices shouted: sounds of surprise, or excitement. Luis and Gloria, sharing Gloria's horse, trotted back to Fernanda. Fernanda waved then looked past them. *Where is Miguel?* She thought. And then, savoring the words, *Where is my love?*

Luis hopped off the horse. "Fernanda, I'll stay with Ignacio and Jorge. Miguel is waiting up ahead. You must go see. It's California. We've reached California!"

She jumped off Aletta and ran, pushing her way forward, saying, "Excuse me, excuse me." She passed Nicolas, who stood next to his horse talking to Ramona.

"Nicolas," Fernanda said. "They say we've reached California. Is it true?"

"Yes. Such a journey, but we've finally arrived in California." The smile on Nicolas's face didn't hide the touch of melancholy in his eyes when he looked at Fernanda.

"It's exciting, isn't it, Fernanda?" Ramona asked. "And Nicolas has news that makes the day even more so." She gazed at him, her eyes filled with pride.

Nicolas flushed and proudly straightened his uniform. "The captain has promoted me to Sergeant. I have a regiment of my own now."

"Nicolas! Congratulations. I'm so happy for you."

"Thank you. Now go. You must see for yourself the reason for our long travels."

Fernanda ran on, glancing back once more at Nicolas and Ramona. They'd returned to their conversation. Perhaps Ramona would finally get her wish. She'd make a good wife for Nicolas, a good military wife as her mother had been and her grandmother as well.

Fernanda found Miguel with others at the edge of a ridge. A path wound down to the valley below with a sparkling river that crisscrossed the lush green floor.

"Miguel," Fernanda called, running toward him.

He swung around and, with shining eyes, grabbed her hand. "Come!"

She followed Miguel down the path, running, skipping, both of them laughing and shouting with joy. Fernanda's head felt light with the realization that she had made it to California, that the dreams and longings in Tubac she could never quite define lay before her—a new life in California.

Gasping, they reached the stream. Fernanda cupped her hands into the cool clear water and drank. Had water ever tasted so sweet? She splashed Miguel. He grinned and did the same to her. She snapped a twig from a bush and breathed in its perfume. "Rosemary." She held it out for Miguel to smell. "And look." Mixed with the rosemary were wild roses covered with dormant buds. She clutched Miguel's hand. "It's a paradise. We should call it Paradise Valley."

Miguel pulled her close. "I arrived in Paradise a week ago, on the day you told me you loved me." He kissed her, his lips still fresh and cool from the stream.

Hearing shouts behind them, they jumped apart. The others trailed down the path, and Captain Anza said they would set up camp next to the river.

That night, the women pulled out their new petticoats, rebozos, and ribbons to celebrate their arrival in California. Alone in the tent, Fernanda dressed for the party. She slipped into her petticoat and skirt. Next she tied a red ribbon at the end of her braid. Reaching for her new rebozo, she remembered she'd given it to Sikul. She saw the corner of Mama's shawl tucked into the bottom of the trunk and pulled it out. As she draped it around her shoulders, she thought of the day

Papa had brought it home for Mama's birthday. A special gift, one they could probably little afford. Mama had protested, but how radiant she looked when he enfolded her in its silky opulence. Fernanda smoothed the material against her arms, feeling the worn, loosened threads of the embroidered butterflies. Tonight, no one would have a more beautiful rebozo than she.

When she joined the party, Papa eyed the shawl, touched it lightly, and then kissed her forehead. He cocked his head, regarding her with a small smile, though also with a touch of sadness.

"Papa, what is it?"

"Oh, sorry, Mi'ja. It's only that you're looking more and more like your mother."

Fernanda threw her arms around her father's neck and whispered, "Thank you" in his ear.

Señor Gonzales called to her, "Let's play some music. Their feet are itching to dance."

Fernanda, the Señor, Miguel, and other guitarists and drummers played while Feliciana sang. The colonists danced and cheered. After several Spanish ballads, Fernanda set aside the guitar, stood, and pulled her father to her side. "Papa," she whispered, "will you join me in a dance I learned from the Yumas? A dance I want to do for Mama?"

Papa squeezed her hand and nodded.

"Please," she called out. "I want to show you a dance. Can you form a circle?"

A few people laughed, and one of the Feliz boys called out, "Fernanda, what strange dance will you have us do?"

"You'll see, our Indian ancestors knew how to celebrate, too."

People shuffled forward, forming a wider and wider circle as more joined in. Her brothers came, Miguel and

Gloria, Feliciana with Estaquia wrapped snugly against her chest, Tomása, and the Gonzales, Feliz, and Gutiérrez families. Ramona hesitated, and then took her sister's hand, and she and her family joined the circle.

Nicolas stood with three other soldiers on the outskirts of the circle. Fernanda wanted so badly to ask him to join. He had loved Mama, too. He'd been friendly enough earlier, but everyone knew of their broken engagement. Would it humiliate him if she approached him and singled him out in front of the others?

And then Miguel walked over to the soldiers. Nicolas's shoulders stiffened. Miguel spoke to him, nodded toward the circle, and gestured at the soldiers. Nicolas crossed his arms, still scowling as Miguel talked some more. But slowly, Nicolas's shoulders and arms and face loosened, and when Miguel held out his hand, Nicolas shook it. Miguel walked back to the circle, and Nicolas and the soldiers found places among the colonists. Nicolas nodded at Fernanda with a small smile on his face, a sad smile, it seemed, but one that told her everything was okay between them. She nodded back, and then put one arm around Papa's shoulders and the other around Gloria's.

"Just follow what I do," she said.

Everyone linked together, arms draped over their neighbor's. Fernanda stomped one foot, then the other, and bent forward at the waist. "That's all. We step in unison around the circle. That's the key: we must all dance as one."

The group followed her lead. One of the colonists beat on a drum, and Miguel broke from the dance to play his flute, both musicians following the rhythm of the dancers' footsteps. Joy lifted Fernanda's feet. Surely Great-grandmother and Mama were celebrating with them from their home in Morning Base.

Some dancers stumbled and collided with each other. Fernanda laughed with the others as the circle broke. Señor Gonzales strummed his guitar, Miguel continued playing, and others grabbed their instruments while the colonists danced as before. Papa bowed and asked Feliciana to dance. Nicolas took Ramona into his arms and led her around the other dancers. Ignacio and Tomása held hands and tried to follow the adults' steps. Luis danced with Gloria.

Fernanda slipped away from the celebration. She strolled for a short distance, breathing in the soft perfume of the surrounding herbs. Laughter and music floated toward her. *They sound so happy*, she thought.

She looked up at the stars that sparked against the black sky and felt the strong presence of her mother. If only Mama could see her now, see how she had changed. *Look at me, Mama. Perhaps I'm not the woman you expected, or hoped I'd be. But I'm happy and excited about my life. I think you'd be happy for me and approve of my choices.*

Fernanda suddenly understood that Mama, too, had made choices. She had lived the life she wanted with her husband, her children, her home. Great-grandmother also did as she wished: living with the Pima traditions, refusing to follow the white man's ways. Now Fernanda would follow her own path, and the life she had longed for would somehow be realized. She'd build a life in Monte Rey that would honor both her Spanish and Pima ancestors.

She suddenly thought of the song Mama had begun to sing that last morning, and remembered now that she had also sung it one spring day when Ignacio was an infant. A Pima song Mama had said, one of the few times she mentioned her Indian past. Fernanda was in the garden caring for her tender seedlings. Mama walked around from the front of the hut, cradling the infant Ignacio in her arms. She smiled at Fernanda, and then snuggled her nose against Ignacio's tummy. She looked up, her face full of joy, and sang the song. A song, she said, the ancient ones sang when they emerged from their journey through the dark center of the earth. A song of happiness and the promise of a fresh start in a shining new world.

Now, as Fernanda listened to her fellow colonists celebrating their arrival in California and she looked ahead to the life she'd share with Papa, her brothers, her love Miguel, and her sister Gloria, the words of her mother's song came to her:

This is the bright land:
We arrive singing,
Head-dresses waving in the breeze.
The land trembles with our dancing and singing.
Singing and dancing, we all rejoice.
We have come! We have come!

Turn the page for exciting facts about the history of the expedition and characters in this story, along with an author's note and glossary of Spanish terms.

Historical Note on the Expedition

Few people have heard about the 1775-1776 Anza expedition from Mexico to California. Maybe because it happened at the same time as another important event: the American Revolution. But the Spanish colonization of California, seventy years before pioneers from the east crossed the Rockies, also helped shape the future of the United States.

By 1775, Spain had quite an empire in the New World. Most of the people of New Spain lived in Mexico, Central America, and South America. The empire also had settlements in present-day Arizona, New Mexico, and Texas, and a few missions and presidios (military posts) in California.

A small number of soldiers and Franciscan priests lived in the presidios and missions. Many times they faced starvation as they waited for supply ships to make the slow journey up the coast from Mexico. Fighting treacherous waters and heavy winds, the ships were often lost at sea or destroyed against rocky cliffs.

Because of this difficulty in getting supplies to the soldiers and priests, and to bring more colonists to California, Spanish rulers wished to discover an overland route from Mexico to California. In 1774, King Carlos III authorized Captain Juan Bautista de Anza to lead an expedition in the hopes of finding this route. After a three-month journey, Anza arrived in San Gabriel, having discovered a safe passage across the desert and over the mountains to California.

With this success, the king ordered Anza to lead another expedition, this time bringing with him colonists and the supplies they would need to start lives in the new territory. Most of the colonists who signed on for the journey were poor.

They hoped for a better life in California and were enticed by the new clothes, arms, household goods, and horses given to them by order of the Spanish king.

Lieutenant Luis Joaquin Moraga and Sergeant Juan Pablo Grijalba assisted Captain Anza. Three priests also accompanied the expedition. Father Pedro Font recorded the latitudes in his diary, adding descriptions of the Indians, weather, land, and more. Fathers Antonio Garcés and Tomás Eixarch traveled only as far as the Colorado River where they stayed to teach the Yuma Indians Christianity. Father Garcés and Captain Anza also kept diaries of the journey.

Thirteen muleteers packed and unpacked the mules, laden with the travelers' supplies, at each campsite. Three vaqueros kept the herd of cattle together, which would be used for meat on the journey and the presidios in California. Anza and each of the priests had servants. Three Indian interpreters helped communicate with the Pimas, Yumas, and other tribes. (Please see the Author's Note below for more information on the Indians.) In all, there were 240 people (including 115 children ranging in age from infant to eighteen), 695 horses and mules, and 355 head of cattle.

The expedition began in Culiacán, Sinaloa, Mexico in March 1775, where Anza recruited the first colonists, adding more between there and Tubac. They spent the summer in Horcasitas, at that time the capital of the state of Sonora, left there September 29 and, after traveling for three weeks, arrived at Tubac, the presidio Anza commanded. (This is where my novel Yakimali's Gift begins.) There, more colonists signed on, and the expedition left again on October 23, 1775. The journey from Culiacán, Mexico to Monterey, California would cover almost 2000 miles and last almost one year.

The colonists survived extreme conditions and hardship along the trail: death, births, heat, dust storms, wind, rain, snow, dying animals, and limited supplies. Still, life continued. Three couples were married. Eight women gave birth, although only three of the babies lived and one woman died in childbirth.

The expedition crossed over into California on January 1, 1776 (where Yakimali's Gift ends) and arrived at the San Gabriel mission on January 4. Anza left the colonists there for over one month while he joined a confrontation between soldiers and Indians at the San Diego mission. The captain returned to San Gabriel, and on February 21, 1776, Anza and those colonists who hadn't settled in San Gabriel set off for Monterey and arrived there on March 10. Those colonists who had started in Culiacán traveled just a few days short of one year.

Feliciana, the young widow who befriends Fernanda in *Yakimali's Gift*, was a real person who joined Juan Bautista de Anza's expedition from Mexico to California. In Feliciana's world of eighteenth century Mexico, women of all classes were expected to be modest, unassertive, and devoted to God and home. Women did have a certain amount of freedom to choose their husbands since parents and the Catholic church wanted the marriages to last. (They lost some of that freedom when, in 1778, a proclamation from Spain required parental consent for marriages of people under the age of twenty-five.)

Even though women could choose their husbands, there was a strict class structure in place, and mixed marriages were frowned upon. Children of mixed-race couples had specific labels. The most common were mestizo (Spanish and Indian), mulatto (Spanish and African), coyote (mestizo and Indian), and castizo (Spanish and mestizo). People claimed the name of "Spaniard" when they could get away with it, even if they didn't have pure Spanish blood.

It's believed that Feliciana came from "pure" Spanish ancestry, thus her parents disapproved of her marriage to Jose Gutierrez, a mestizo. They had two daughters, Tomasa and Estaquia. Possibly to escape the strict Mexican society, Feliciana and Jose, who was a soldier under Anza's command, decided to join the expedition. However, before they were to depart, Jose was killed in an Indian attack. Still, Feliciana, with her two young daughters, chose to go on the journey.

With her spirit, bravery, and strong will, she embraced the opportunity to build a life for herself and her children in California. Much to the dismay of Father Pedro Font, a priest on the expedition and who was against Feliciana joining the expedition, she helped buoy the spirits of her traveling companions when, for example, she sang at a fandango, or dance, the colonists enjoyed on the expedition.

In his diary, Font wrote:

At night, with the joy at the arrival of all the people, they held a fandango here. It was somewhat discordant, and a very bold widow who came with the expedition sang some verses which were not at all nice, applauded and cheered by all the crowd.

Besides her two daughters, Tomasa and Estaquia, from her first marriage to Jose Gutierrez, Feliciana had seven more children with her second husband, Juan Francisco Lopez. Many of her descendants, showing the same courage and conviction as Feliciana, became important figures in California history.

In 1841, the Spanish government granted Feliciana's daughter, Maria Ignacia Lopez Carrillo, more than 8000 acres in what is now Santa Rosa in northern California. Her husband had died at the age of forty-three, and Ignacia was one of only a few unmarried women to receive such a grant. She obviously inherited Feliciana's spirit since she managed the rancho herself, not something a woman of that period typically did.

Benicia, the California capital in 1853-1854, was named after Feliciana's granddaughter, Francisca Benicia Carrillo de Vallejo. Francisca Benicia was the wife of General Mariano Guadalupe Vallejo, a prominent Mexican military and political leader in California in the years after Mexico won its independence from Spain (1821), and during the Mexican-American war (1846-1848).

Two grandsons (sons of Feliciana's infant on the Anza expedition, Estaquia) were very involved in the politics of their time. Andrés Pico was the Commander-in-Chief of the Mexican military during the Mexican-American War. He and American Lieutenant-Colonel John C. Fremont signed the Treaty of Cahuenga, which ended the war. Andrés' brother, Pío Pico, was the last Mexican governor of California before it became part of the United States in 1850.

Feliciana's great-grandson Romualdo Pacheco became the State of California's first and only Hispanic governor in 1875. Higher education was an important issue for him, and he promoted the establishment of the University of California. Pacheco also served many years in the California State Senate, and when elected to the U.S. House of Representatives, he became the first Hispanic chairman of a standing Congressional committee.

Feliciana left quite a legacy. She probably would have been very proud of her descendants' accomplishments. And, learning of their lives, most likely happy with the decision she made on that September day in 1775 to risk leaving all she knew and making the long trek to California.

On writing *Yakimali's Gift*

Fernanda's story came from a group of short stories I wrote about children telling how and why their ancestors settled in the United States. When I decided to write a novel about Fernanda and the expedition, and delved into the research, I was fascinated to learn that the colonization occurred during the time of the American Revolution and some seventy years before the often-told story of the east-to-west migration of pioneers. This further inspired me to write about this little known, but important, part of California and U.S. history.

The fun part about doing research is digging through layers and layers of information. I started out a bit overwhelmed, with little information and wondering how to tackle the project. I ended up overwhelmed by the amount of information I discovered, wondering how to fit it all into the story.

Fact versus Fiction

Although Fernanda and her story are fictitious, other characters in Yakimali's Gift—Juan Bautista de Anza; the priests Pedro Font, Antonio Garcés, and Tomás Eixarch; Lieutenant Moraga; Sergeant Grijalva; Vicente and Manuela Feliz; Luis and Micaela Gonzales and their children; the Gutierrez family; and Feliciana Maria Arballo and her two children— were all real people who traveled on the expedition. The "Web de Anza" website http://anza.uoregon.edu/ has a wealth of information about the expedition including a Who's Who on the colonists, and the diaries of Anza, Font, and Garcés. The diaries are fascinating to read, particularly Font's "expanded" version. His details can be vivid, and his personal opinions about the Indians and other aspects of the journey give some insight into the Spanish attitudes of the time.

The incidents in Yakimali's Gift follow many of those from the diaries such as the route traveled, encounters with Indians, deaths and illnesses, and the weather.

I did change some events for the sake of the plot. For instance, Anza and the priests rode out to the Casa Grande ruins, but there's no record of any other colonists exploring the ruins. And though the horse races between the Yumas and the colonists are fiction, they did celebrate together as mentioned in Font's diary November 28, 1775 (and in other entries where the Yumas were repeatedly referred to as "festive"):

The Yumas entertained us in an arbor which Captain Palma [the name the Spaniards gave the Yuma leader] had ordered erected here as soon as he learned of our coming, and many Indians of both sexes assembled to visit us, very festive and joyful and very much painted in various modes and colors... On our arrival the soldiers were ordered to fire a few shots to reciprocate the pleasure manifested by these people at our coming. This pleased the Yumas greatly and they responded to the musket–shots with a great shouting and hullabaloo.

Yakimali's Gift ends with the colonists' arrival in California. The expedition continued to San Antonio (California) with many of the travelers settling in San Gabriel, Monterey, and other places along the way. Today, the Juan Bautista de Anza Trail is a National Historic Trail, and many of the original sites along the route still exist. During my research, I visited some of the sites in Arizona: Tubac and the presidio, the missions at San Xavier del Bac and Tumacacori, parts of the Yuma River, and the Casa Grande (a National Monument). I went on this trip after I had already done a lot of book research, and it was a real thrill to see the places that I'd been reading and writing about, and to see first-hand the desert areas where Fernanda would have lived. Luckily, I was there in the spring, so I missed the rains and heat of August!

Women and Children on the Expedition

When I first read about this expedition, I was shocked to learn that several women chose to go even though they were in advanced stages of pregnancy. I wanted to know more about the women and their children who made up more than half the number of colonists. The diaries of Anza, Font, and Garcés give just cursory mention of the women's experience, and almost nothing about the children. For instance, Anza briefly writes about the death of a woman during childbirth on the first night of the journey, October 24, 1775, without even mentioning her name (which was Manuela Feliz), and then goes on to talk about the weather:

At three o'clock in the morning, it not having been possible by means of the medicines which had been applied in the previous hours, to remove the afterbirth from our mother, other various troubles befell her. As a result she was taken with paroxysms of death, and after the sacraments of penance and extreme unction had been administered to her, with the aid of the fathers who accompany us she rendered up her spirit at a quarter to four. At seven o'clock today it began to rain, and continued until half past ten...

Who was the woman? Did she have other children? How did the death that occurred on that first night affect the other colonists? These questions and more intrigued me. Reading one of my resources, Women and the Conquest of California by Virginia M. Bouvier, further inspired me to look at the expedition through the eyes of women and children.

With limited information available, I began to imagine what life was like on that first march along the Anza trail—who the people were and why they had left their homes to emigrate to California. Thus the story of Fernanda and her journey was born. Though her life, her family, her connection with the Pima Indians and the old Pima woman, Sikul, are all fictitious, I created Fernanda's story based on facts about that period of history found in the resources listed in a bibliography on my website http://lindacovella.com/yakimalis-gift/bibliography/. There, I added a short description of each book should you like to read more about the period and journey yourself.

Race in 18th century New Spain and the Spanish/Indian Relationship

Just as we see today, there were race issues in 18th century Mexico, New Spain, and that interested me as well in writing my story. Most people of mixed heritage (typically Spanish and Indian) wished to be named Spaniard. Those with the "purest" Spanish blood enjoyed many societal privileges, thus people often claimed to have more Spanish ancestry than they actually did.

Classes were categorized and named according to what a group's heritage mix was: People with one Spanish parent and one Indian parent were called Mestizo; people of Indian/Mestizo mix were called Coyote; Indian/Coyote were classified as Indian.

I didn't research Apaches since they don't play a big part in the story. But I was surprised that the expedition never encountered any Apaches since many historical records show them as an ever-present threat to other Indian tribes and to colonists. This could possibly have been because the travelers and animals were well guarded by the soldiers and vaqueros.

I did have difficulty, though, locating writings from the perspective of the Pimas, Papagos, and Yumas. And information about the relationship between the soldiers, missionaries, and Indians during that time is sketchy as compared to books available about these relationships in California and at the California missions. There was a campaign of course by the Catholic Jesuits and later the Franciscans to convert the Indians. But the Yumas and Pimas the colonists encountered were largely as yet not converted, much to the priests' dismay. The Indians' minimal clothing (and often nakedness) especially bothered the priests and embarrassed the colonists. The priests encouraged the Indians to wear Spanish-style clothes, but few Indians did unless they lived at the missions, which became more prominent after the Anza expedition, especially in California.

After much digging, I found some wonderful books that detailed the different tribes' housing, clothing, religious beliefs, language, and social customs of that time. These books are also listed in the bibliography on my website.

Parts of the story that the old Pima woman, Sikul (a fictitious character), tells Fernanda are based on fact, particularly the "uprising" of the Pimas. The conflict between the Pimas, the Jesuits, and the Spanish soldiers occurred in 1751 when Papa would have been sixteen, Mama four, and Fernanda yet to be born nine years later. There's been much debate throughout history as to the cause of the fight. I had only uncovered the most basic facts about the conflict when I came across Russell Charles Ewing's dissertation The Pima Uprising, 1751-1752 (see bibliography on my website). Although his narrative can be construed as being biased on the side of the soldiers and the Catholic Church, he gives a lot of otherwise hard-to-find details about the circumstances before, during, and after the conflict, as well as further insight into the Spanish/Indian relationship of that time.

In subsequent years, beyond the time in which Yakimali's Gift takes place, as the population of the California missions increased and the Spanish continued their efforts to Christianize the Indians, the relationship between the Spaniards and the indigenous people worsened. I'll explore this and the impact of the California missions on the Indians in the sequel to Yakimali's Gift when Fernanda will again confront conflicts arising from her mixed Spanish and Pima Indian heritage.

Celebrate Your Heritage. Live Your Passion

In the end, I wanted Yakimali's Gift to be a story of hope. Hope that we value our ancestry and appreciate the richness of our country's diversity. And hope that, like Fernanda, we have the determination and passion to live the lives we truly desire among the people we love.

~Linda Covella

November 2014

Yakimali's Gift Discussion Questions

What are some of the book's themes? How important are they?

How would you describe Fernanda's outlook on her life in the beginning of the story, and how does that outlook change by the end of her journey; how has Fernanda grown?

Do you think Fernanda has a good relationship with her mother? Her father? Describe those relationships.

What role does Feliciana play in Fernanda's life?

What are some of the ways Fernanda's perspective on the Indians change along the journey?

Fernanda is torn between Nicolas and Miguel. What are some good and bad qualities of each man?

How do Miguel and Nicolas grow/change by the end of the journey?

How are the racial conflicts portrayed in the story similar to those of today?

Fernanda is confronted with two religions, one from her Spanish background and one from her Pima Indian background. Describe some of the differences and similarities of the two religions.

How significant is the butterfly symbol to the plot or characters?

How does the setting figure into the book?

How would the book have been different if it had taken place in a different time or place?

About the Author

Linda Covella's varied job experience and education (associate degrees in art, business and mechanical drafting & design, a BS degree in Manufacturing Management) have led her down many paths and enriched her life experiences. But one thing she never strayed from is her love of writing.

Her first official publication was a restaurant review column in a local newspaper. But when she published articles for various children's magazines, she realized she'd found her niche, writing for children and teens. She hopes to bring to kids and teens the feelings books gave her when she was young: the worlds they opened, the things they taught, the feelings they expressed.

No matter what new paths Linda may travel down, she sees her writing as a lifelong joy and commitment.

Linda lives in Santa Cruz, CA with her husband and dog Ginger.

Learn more about Linda and her writing at
http://lindacovella.com/

To subscribe to her newsletter for books news, interviews, contests and more, email
linda.covella@rocklogic.com
with "newsletter" in the subject.

Glossary of Spanish Words

agua (AH-gwah) Water.

amigo (ah-MEE-goh) Friend.

amor (ah-MOHR) Love. (te amo (TAY ah-MOH) I love you).

atole (ah-TOH-lay) A drink, served hot or at room temperature, made with corn (or cornmeal) and water or milk, and can be flavored with sugar, cinnamon, chocolate, or fruits. Atole, an ancient Mesoamerican food, is still enjoyed in Mexico today, especially on the Day of the Dead (Día de los Muertos), which also originated in ancient times and today is celebrated on November 1st and 2nd.

bonita (boh-NEE-tah) Pretty. (bonito: masculine form of pretty: handsome).

buenos dias (BWAY-nos DEE-ahs) Good morning. A greeting used until twelve noon.

caballo (cah-BAH-yoh) Horse.

castizo (cah-STEE-soh) One of the racial classifications of 18th century New Spain, a castizo was born of mestizo and a Spaniard. If someone was born of a castizo and a Spaniard, he or she was considered a Spaniard.

cigarro (see-GAH-rroh) Cigarette. In mid-18th century New Spain, men, women, and even children smoked. They carried paper wrappers, tobacco, flint, steel, and cotton wick in a paper or tin box. Wealthier people had special boxes decorated with gold, silver, and jewels. Cigarros were offered to guests along with cocoa. For special guests, women would light the cigarro, take the first puff, and then give it to the guest. It was considered rude if the guest refused the cigarro.

coyote (co-YO-tay) One of the racial classifications of 18th century New Spain, a coyote was born of a mestizo and an Indian.

culebra (coo-LAY-brah) Snake. (culebra de agua: water snake. Besides the name of an actual snake, this term was used to describe devastating thunderstorms that could flood and destroy entire villages).

duros (DOO-rohs) Hard. (see peso).

fandango (fahn-DAHN-goh) A dance, or the music accompanying the dance. The fandango, one of the oldest dances of Spain, was a courtship dance where the man and woman faced each other and danced without touching, clacking castanets, snapping their fingers, and stomping their feet (a form of flamenco). Later, in Mexico, fandango became a general term for dance.

Feliz Navidad (fay-LEES nah-bee-DAHD) Merry Christmas.

galleta (gah-YAY-tah) Cracker or cookie.

hediondilla (AY-dee-ohn-DEE-yah) This is a shrub found in the deserts of the Southwestern United States. Another name is creosote bush. It has resinous leaves and small yellow flowers. In Spanish, hediondilla means "little stinker," although some people enjoy the smell of the plant.

hermano (ehr-MAH-noh) Brother. (hermana: sister)

hola (OH-lah) Hello

laguna (lah-GOO-nah) Lake (laguna del hospital (ohs-pee-TAHL) Hospital lake)

madores (mah-DOHR-ays) At the Sonoran missions in mid-18th century New Spain, the madores were Indians who supervised the grown children and arranged their marriages, pairing the ones that they felt were most suited to each other. The madores also cared for the sick.

mestizo (may-STEE-soh) One of the racial classifications of 18th century New Spain, a mestizo was born of an Indian and a Spaniard.

metate (may-TAH-tay) A stone used to grind corn. Pfefferkorn described it as "a flat, somewhat roughened stone, which is three to three-and-one-half feet long and about two feet wide. This is the millstone on which, with the aid of another stone, likewise roughened, the maize [corn] is ground." This would be similar to a mortar and pestle.

mi (mee) My.

mi'ja (MEE-hah) This is an endearment, a contraction of mi hija (mee EE-hah) meaning "my daughter."

mi'jo (MEE-hoh) My son. See mi'ja.

muchacho (moo-CHAH-choh) Boy. (muchacha: Girl).

mulatto One of the racial classifications of 18th century New Spain, a mulatto was born of a Black and a Spaniard.

mula (MOO-lah) Mule. (mulo: masculine form—a male mule)

niño(s) (nee-NYOH) Masculine form of child (children) niña Feminine form.

peso (PEH-soh) The peso is the currency used in Mexico and some Central American and South American countries. The peso originated in Spain during the time of Ferdinand and Isabel in 1497, but today Spain uses the euro for its currency. The word "peso" means "weight" in Spanish. Pesos duros, in mid-18th century New Spain, referred to the silver coins minted in Mexico.

pobrecito (POH-bray-SEE-toh) Poor little boy. (pobrecita: poor little girl).

por favor (pohr fah-BOHR) Please.

posole (poh-SOH-lay) A soup made from corn kernels and flavored with pork or other meat and various vegetables and hot sauce. Like atole, posole, also spelled "posole," is an ancient Mesoamerican food and is still enjoyed in Mexico today. You can find it on menus in many Mexican and Spanish food restaurants.

potra (POH-dra) Filly—a young female horse.

presidio (preh-SEE-dee-oh) The presidios were military posts or garrisons used to protect the missions and settlements as the Spaniards expanded their frontier from central Mexico into California. The presidios were usually built with logs or adobe bricks. Storage facilities, a chapel, and housing for soldiers were constructed within a high wall with only a front gate, and sometimes a rear one, for entrance and exit. Taking advantage of the soldiers' protection, settlers built homes and planted crops near the presidios.

pueblo (PWAY-bloh) Village or town.

querida (kay- REE-dah) Beloved.

rábanos (RAH-bah-nos) Radishes.

rebozo (ray-BOH-soh) A shawl women in New Spain wore usually over their heads, or across their shoulders, as adornment and as protection from the weather. Some historians also believe the rebozo was worn for reasons of modesty, a tradition possibly brought from Spain and started during the time of the Moors, Muslim inhabitants of medieval Spain.

señor (say-NYOHR) Mister.

señora (say-NYOH-rah) Mrs. (Title for a married woman).

señorita (say-nyoh-REE-tah) Miss (Title for an unmarried woman).

sí (see) Yes.

tiempo (tee-EHM-poh) Time. (tiempo de aguas literally means "time of waters" but can be translated as "rainy season").

vaquero (bah-KAY-roh) Cowboy. The American cowboy originated from the vaqueros who started the cowboy tradition in 16th century New Spain when Spaniards brought horses to the new world.

viejo (bee-AY-hoh) Old.

www.ingramcontent.com/pod-product-compliance
Lightning Source LLC
Chambersburg PA
CBHW070605120726
47909CB00007B/2441